This series is a unique collaboration between three award-winning authors, Adèle Geras, Linda Newbery and Ann Turnbull, all writing about one very special house and the extraordinary girls and women who have lived there throughout history.

This collection first published in the USA in 2019 by Usborne Publishing Ltd.,
Usborne House, 83-85 Saffron Hill, London EC1N 8RT, England. www.usborne.com

A CIP catalogue record for this book is available from the British Library.

JFMAMJJ SOND/20 05703/2 ISBN: 9780794548346 ALB: 9781601304865

Printed in China.

Girls at War

ANN TURNBULL

For my mother

Contents

6 Chelsea Walk, 1941

Basement

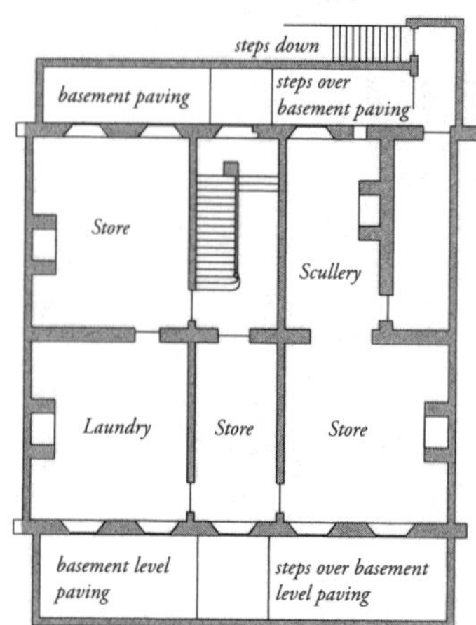

First-floor apartment

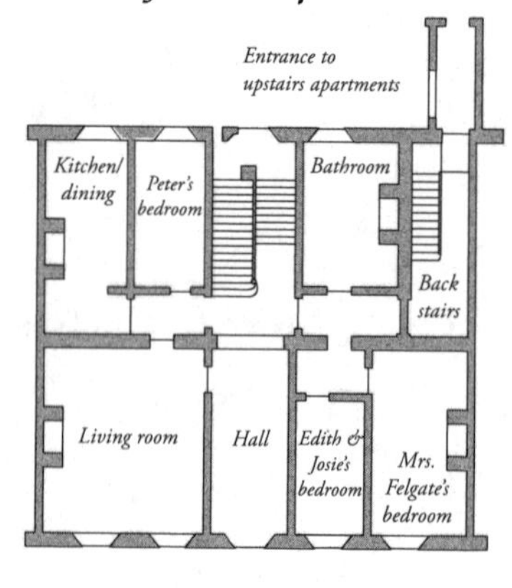

Second-floor apartment

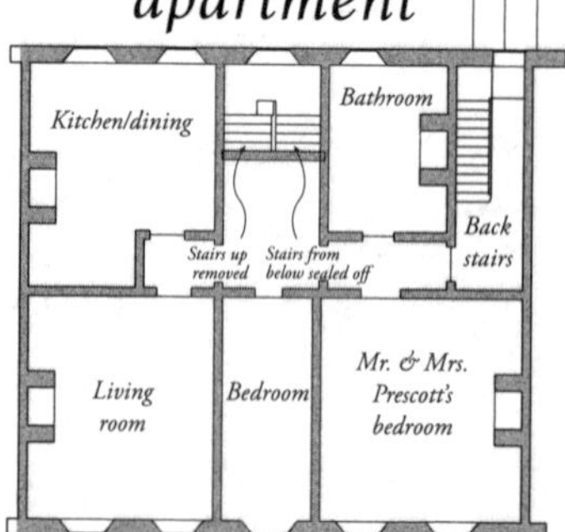

Third-floor apartment

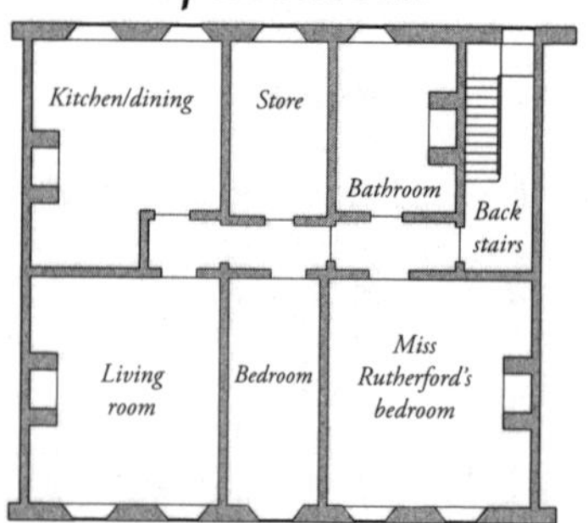

Roof space

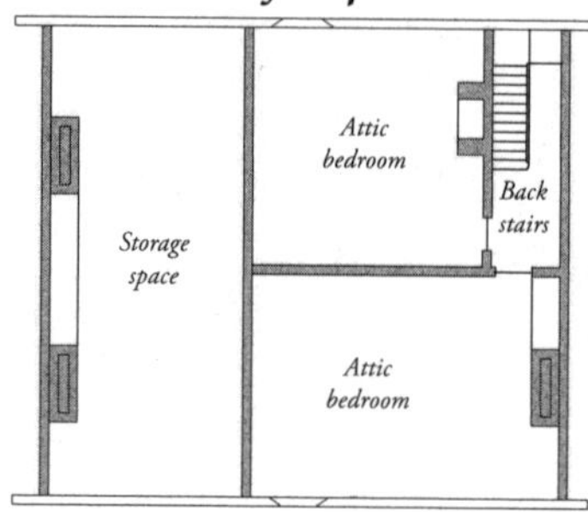

Chapter One

A Move to Chelsea

The house had changed. Silly, of course, to have expected it to look the same, but Josie remembered it from visits before the war began: a big five-story house of red brick, solid and strong – a house that looked as if it would remain unchanged forever.

The bushes in the garden had been hacked back, revealing a surprisingly large space in which spring cabbages and onions were growing. A few daffodils showed tight yellow buds. Josie looked up and saw that every one of the windows was crisscrossed with brown sticky tape.

Her mother opened the gate and they carried Josie's suitcase up a short flight of stone steps to the front door. Josie glanced down into the basement area and saw sandbags piled against the walls. The windows were boarded up.

"Is that where they shelter?" she asked. At home in Greenwich she and her mother had an Anderson shelter in the garden.

"I think so." Her mother looked momentarily anxious before she said, in a bracing tone, "You'll be just as safe here as at Granny's. Safer, probably. And you'll be with Edith. You'll enjoy that."

"Yes."

But it would be strange, Josie thought, staying with her cousin. She'd often visited for the day, but never stayed. And although the families had always been friendly it might be different now, because of Ted.

"Do they know?" she asked. "About Ted? Does Edith know?"

"We told Aunty Grace and Uncle Walter. I doubt if they'd tell Edith. And Aunty Grace wouldn't gossip. The neighbors won't know."

No, thought Josie, Aunty Grace was always polite and correct. And if she felt differently about Josie now, she wouldn't show it. But Edith…?

The doorbell was labeled "Felgate." It was the only one because the tenants of the upstairs apartments used the back entrance. Her mother pressed the bell.

The door opened, and Josie's aunt was there, and Edith beside her, and behind them the grand, high-ceilinged hall with its floor of black and white marble tiles.

Aunty Grace gave Josie her cool kiss that smelled of face powder. "My goodness, Josie, you've grown!" she said.

Josie blushed. She seemed to be growing fast these days, and preferred it not to be commented on. She glanced at her cousin, who was also twelve. Edith did look bigger, and her face was less chubby and childish, but she still had that prettiness – dark curls and a dimple when she smiled – that Josie, with her straight fair hair and glasses, had always envied.

Aunty Grace drew Josie's mother toward the kitchen, where they chatted as the kettle was put on to boil.

Biddy, the Felgates' little black cat, crept out into the hall, and Edith scooped her up. "Here's Josie who's come to see you."

Josie stroked the cat. Her own pet, a spaniel named Russ, was being looked after by a neighbor in Greenwich, and she knew she would miss him.

Edith smiled at Josie over the cat's head. "You can come to my school," she said. "Mummy arranged it with Miss Hallam."

"Is she your teacher?"

"Yes. There are only two left now, Miss Hallam and Miss Gregory. All the others have joined the Services.

And a lot of the girls were evacuated and haven't come back. We just go in the mornings."

Josie thought of her school in Greenwich. That was only part-time, too, but it was enough. She remembered the name calling, the way she was shut out of things, the way even some of the teachers had cooled toward her. Surely it would be better here, among strangers?

"Come and have some tea, girls!" Edith's mother called.

They followed her into the enormous oak-paneled living room with its expanse of carpet in dark floral patterns. Biddy escaped from Edith's arms and made straight for the hearthrug in front of the fire.

Josie, looking around, remembered that in the past this room had always had tall vases of cut flowers in it, whatever was in season; Aunty Grace had a regular order at the florist's. Not now. There were no flowers at all, and the pale damask curtains that framed the long windows were half-hidden behind bulky blackout drapes.

On the mantelpiece were several framed family photographs. Josie's eyes were drawn to one of a smiling young man: her cousin Peter, Edith's brother. Peter wore flying goggles pushed up over his leather helmet, and a padded jacket with the collar turned out to reveal its fleece lining; the straps of a parachute harness could be seen around his shoulders and hips; and behind him was his plane – a Spitfire. Josie glanced at her mother and saw that she too had seen the photograph.

A fire was burning in the grate, and tea was laid on a low table: china cups, white napkins, even some biscuits. They sat down, and Aunty Grace handed out little rose-patterned plates. Josie immediately felt anxious that she might drop crumbs or say something insufficiently polite. The Felgates were so formal, so stilted in their conversation. And yet Edith, she remembered, had always been a secretly disobedient child, bubbling under the polite surface, much naughtier than Josie once their parents were out of sight. Would she have changed?

"Pass Josie another cookie, Edith," Aunty Grace said.

The cookies were not as good as they looked. They tasted dry; one of those fat-free recipes from *The Kitchen Front*, Josie guessed.

Nevertheless, cookies were cookies, and she and Edith ate several each while their mothers talked about Josie's grandmother, who had fallen in the blackout and broken her hip. She needed her daughter to come and stay for a few weeks – which was why Josie was here.

Josie sensed Edith's impatience as she waited for a pause in the conversation. When it came she asked her mother, "May I show Josie our room?"

"Yes, of course, dear. Run along."

It was a relief to leave. They went across the hall and into the small bedroom that until recently Edith had shared with her sister Moira. Josie had always liked her cousins' room. It was pretty, with a white-painted dressing table and pink comforters – a proper girls' room that made her own bedroom at home seem ordinary. Josie's mother didn't bother much about the house. She had always worked from home as a freelance journalist, and throughout her childhood Josie had been aware of the disapproval of some of the neighbors: married women were supposed to devote themselves to home and family. Until now. Now it was different, and her mother had told her that even Aunty Grace worked, unpaid, for the WVS.

"You can have Moira's bed," said Edith.

"Where is she now?" Josie knew Moira had joined the WAAF a few weeks ago.

"East Anglia. Mummy's worrying about her. And about Peter, of course."

She moved to shut the bedroom door. "Want to see something?"

"What?"

Edith opened the armoire and reached deep inside. She brought out what looked like a drawstring shoe bag made of striped sheeting. "Have a look."

The bag was full of shrapnel from bomb sites. There were several bullets. Josie took them out and weighed them in her hand. They were heavy, dull silver, dented where they'd hit the ground. There was some glass, too, fragments of stained-glass window in deep reds and blues.

"That's from the Catholic church," said Edith. "There was a massive hit. All the people sheltering in the crypt were killed. Hilda Rodway – she goes to my school – her cousin was in there."

Josie brought out some small sheared-off bits of metal – and then a watch with a shattered face, stopped at a quarter past six.

"That's when the bomb went off," said Edith. Josie could see that her cousin was particularly proud of this souvenir.

"How horrible." But there was a fascination about the watch, about the thought of that moment when time stopped for someone.

Edith put the things away and hid the bag in the

armoire. "Don't tell Mummy. I'm not allowed to collect shrapnel."

Edith hasn't changed, Josie thought. She wondered what they would do together in the afternoons, when they weren't at school. She remembered, from family visits, climbing the walnut tree in the back garden and, in autumn, collecting the nuts, some to be eaten fresh and the rest pickled. In colder weather they had played in the strange, dead-end space at the top of the stairs – a space that had always fascinated Josie.

Edith seemed to guess her thoughts. "Let's go up to the landing."

They went into the hall and through the archway to what had once been the grand staircase, the center of a big house. Now the stairs, although richly carpeted in Turkish red, led nowhere. The girls ran up them, reached a landing, turned the corner and faced three steps that stopped at a blank wall. Beyond that wall, Josie knew, was the second-floor apartment.

The Felgate children had always made the landing

a play space, though Aunty Grace had worried about them falling downstairs. There were still boxes of *Ludo* and *Snakes and Ladders* on the top step, some *Girls' Own* annuals, and an open box full of toy soldiers. Aunty Grace had encouraged quiet games here. But sometimes, when Josie visited, Edith would fetch shawls and fans from the dressing-up box in her bedroom, and the two of them would parade up and down the great staircase, pretending to be the Victorian ladies who once lived here. Or the landing would become a stage and they'd persuade the older ones – Peter, Ted and Moira – to put on plays with them. Often, though, they would just sit in the hidey-hole at the top and chat and giggle, which is what they did now.

"Who's in your class at school?" Josie asked. "What are they like?"

"Clare Barrington, Pam Denham: they're my friends. Nina Parton; Sylvia Wells; Iris Gray... They're all quite good sorts except Alice Hampton: she's peculiar."

"What sort of peculiar?"

"Oh, teacher's pet. Brainy. No one likes her. We're mixed ages, ten to thirteen, because of the war and doubling up the classes. Part of the school got bombed; we've had *tons* of bombing—"

"So have we!" exclaimed Josie, not to be outdone.

"And we've had to go part-time," Edith continued, "because there's not enough shelter space for all of us. But Miss Hallam's nice. And it's good fun in the air raids. We do quizzes and plays and things."

It'll be so much better here, Josie thought. Edith's my cousin and she'll be my friend. And no one will turn against me because they won't know about Ted.

Edith had begun fiddling with the toy soldiers. She took a few out and stood them on the stair. She glanced sidelong at Josie. "Is Ted a pacifist?" she asked.

And Josie realized that Edith *did* know.

Chapter Two

Family Shame

"I think so," she said. And added, in a rush, "What have they told you?"

"Nothing," said Edith. "No one ever tells *me* anything. Only last time Daddy was home on leave I heard him and Mummy talking about Ted. Something about pacifists and 'Able-bodied young men ought to be doing their bit' – that's what Daddy said. And Mummy said, 'Poor Winifred. It must be so hard for her…'"

"It is," said Josie. She thought of the family discussions that had often turned into arguments. Her father and Ted had both worn the white poppy to show that they were against the war, but once it started her father had felt he had no choice but to join up. "I can't let others fight for me," he'd said.

Ted had passionately disagreed. "People on both sides must refuse to fight. If we all refuse—"

"It's too late," his father said. "And we are up against an evil regime."

"I can't accept that all Germans are evil."

Josie, knowing her father would be going away to fight and Ted might go to prison, felt torn by the arguments.

"They must each do what they feel is right," her mother said, but Josie knew she was distressed.

Later, when her father had gone and Ted was summoned to a tribunal, Josie and her mother felt the hostility of neighbors who had always rather disapproved of the family. Now, even some of her parents' friends deserted them; and at school Josie was first taunted, then ignored. When the Blitz started, and people were being killed, it got worse.

She couldn't hide the tremor in her voice as she told Edith, "It's hard for me, too."

Edith's eyes widened. "Don't worry. I don't blame *you*. I just want to know."

"He's a conscientious objector," said Josie. "When he went to his tribunal they said he could work on the land. He's in forestry. He was sent to Dorset first; then Cheshire." She remembered how, when Ted came home on leave, she had shouted at him, "I hate you! No one at school will speak to me because of you!" But now Edith's father's scathing words made her determined to defend Ted. "He's doing work of national importance," she said.

"But he doesn't risk his life, does he?" said Edith. "Not like Peter."

Peter. Edith's brother was a Spitfire pilot, about the most impressive thing you could be: alone, in his plane, fighting the Hun in the skies above Britain, perhaps with death only moments away. Peter was a hero.

I wish *my* brother was a hero, Josie thought. She loved Ted so much, but he'd left her feeling hurt and confused. She didn't really understand when he told her how he felt he could not be part of what he called "the war machine." Or rather, she did understand when he explained it, but afterwards she listened to all the other voices talking about sacrifice, and heroism, and pulling together, and standing firm; and then it seemed as if Ted had simply found a coward's way out. Especially when the bombs rained down and men like Peter were fighting to destroy the bombers before they got through.

That was what the neighbors thought, back home in Greenwich. Most of them didn't say much; it was the looks; and the way that whenever something scarce came into the grocer's, like soap, or tinned peaches, somehow there was never any left when her mother reached the counter. And they couldn't shop anywhere else; the ration books had their local shop's name, *Hollamby & Son, 27 Albert Road*, printed on them; they had had to get Josie's changed temporarily so that she could bring it here to Chelsea.

"Daddy said this country would already have been invaded if everyone was like Ted," said Edith.

Josie had heard Ted himself answer that one. "If everyone was like him," she said, "there wouldn't be any wars."

"Yes, there would," said Edith, "because everyone wouldn't be like him. Hitler wouldn't, would he?"

"Well, my father's in the army," said Josie.

It was true, but no answer, and she felt she'd betrayed Ted.

Her mother's voice came from the hall. "Josie! Are you up there?"

Josie jumped up and hurried down the stairs, relieved to end the conversation.

"I've got to go now," her mother said. "Have to fetch

Granny from the hospital. Now, I've given your ration book to Aunty Grace, and you've got everything you need in your suitcase. I've put writing paper and envelopes in it. You'll write to me and Granny, won't you?"

Josie nodded. She was thinking more about Russ than Granny. Would he be pining for her?

"Be a good girl, then."

They hugged each other, and then her mother turned to Aunty Grace, thanked her, and began gathering up her coat, umbrella and gas mask. She went down the path, looking lonely and resolute. Josie knew she hated the two of them being separated. With the bombs falling, she was uneasy whenever they were apart. Josie had been evacuated early in the war to a village in Hertfordshire. She'd been unhappy there, had come home and, when she refused to go away again, had sensed her mother's relief. It was one thing her mother and Aunty Grace agreed on. Edith had never been sent away at all.

"Come and unpack your suitcase, Josie," said her

aunt. "Edith, I hope you made some space in your armoire."

Josie had not brought much: her school uniform skirt and blazer, two blouses, an argyle pullover and cardigan, a blue woolen dress that was beginning to feel tight. And underwear: three of everything. In the bottom of the suitcase she had packed a film magazine special, *Black Beauty*, *Jane Eyre* and *The Three Musketeers*.

"Are you going to read all those?"

Edith never seemed to read much. In fact Josie had noticed before that there were very few books in the Felgates' house, except binders full of back numbers of *Good Housekeeping* and big books with titles like *A Wonder Book for Boys and Girls* which were a mixture of stories and things to do. Josie could not explain that she had brought the books for comfort; she liked to dip into them and read parts of them over and over again. She put them on the floor by her bed.

Her aunt was sorting and putting away the clothes in Edith's armoire.

"Come and see the garden," said Edith.

They went out of the back door and down the steps, past the sandbagged sides of the cellar.

As with the front garden, the lawn and flower beds had been taken over to grow vegetables. But there was space for only a few rows because the huge old walnut tree half filled the garden. Josie remembered the great circle of shade it cast in summer, and the harvest of nuts in autumn. Her cousins had told her that the tree was nearly a hundred years old. It was too big now, out of scale, and yet the garden would be ordinary without it.

"Let's climb the tree," said Edith.

The ridged trunk rose to a height above their heads without forking, but Peter had tied a rope to the lowest branch, and this helped them as they began to climb. Josie looked up at the spreading network of bare branches. Edith, above her, had reached the second-floor window level; Josie stopped just below. The tree still towered above them – as high as the attics.

Josie glanced at the windows of the middle apartment.

"Do that old man and woman still live there?" she asked. She remembered them giving her sweets before the war – striped peppermints and cough drops.

"Mr. and Mrs. Prescott? Yes. And Miss Rutherford's on the top floor. She's the ARP warden for our street."

"What's *she* like?"

"Fairly old – about like Mummy. She's a spinster."

Clearly Miss Rutherford was of no interest. Josie climbed to a higher branch and let her legs dangle. "I love this tree."

"Remember when the boys used to try and scare us?" Edith reached out and grabbed Josie's foot.

"Don't!" shrieked Josie.

Edith laughed and began shaking the branch; Josie retaliated, and they both squealed in mock terror.

Before long, Aunty Grace appeared at the back door and signaled to them to come down. They obeyed promptly.

"Not so much noise, please – right outside Mrs. Prescott's window! Remember it's Sunday. In fact, we should be getting ready for church." She turned to Edith. "Come and help me put up the blackout. It'll be dark when we get back."

Josie followed Edith into her bedroom and watched as she drew the heavy black curtains across the pink flowered ones and made sure that no chink of light would show. The apartment was already in darkness when all the rooms were done. They put on their coats and hats, and Aunty Grace slipped a flashlight into her pocket as they went out.

A small movement of people was converging on the Old Church, which was five minutes' walk away, along the Embankment. Two huge barrage balloons, floating high above the river, caught the last gleams of the setting sun. The river slapped softly against the river walk. Josie could smell its salty tang, mixed with the smoke from innumerable coal fires. She thought of it winding eastward, to Greenwich, and to Dagenham, where her mother would be now, in Granny's tiny apartment.

"This is the oldest church in Chelsea," Aunty Grace said to Josie. "It goes back to the fourteenth century. Sir Thomas More worshipped here, in the time of Henry the Eighth."

The church showed no light from outside, but inside gas lamps and candles gave a warm glow. Aunty Grace nodded to various people, then shunted the girls into a pew.

Josie sat on the hard wooden seat and looked around at the congregation: old people, mostly, huddled in coats – many of them fur – against the chill rising up from the stone-flagged floor. She had not often been in a church. Her parents did not go, although Ted now had pacifist friends who did. She gazed at the ancient stonework, the monuments around the walls, the stone figures and draperies. So old! Strange to think of people gathering here hundreds of years ago, looking at those same carvings; people perhaps in danger, as now.

Edith nudged her, and she heard the movement as everyone stood up, and the rustle of hymn books.

She rose, found her place, and began to sing.

When they left, it was dark outside. Some people switched on flashlights, but held them pointing downward. Josie knew everyone would be hoping for a quiet night, with no bombing. When the Blitz had begun, last September, there was bombing every night for weeks, but these last few months it had been quieter and they had usually been able to sleep in their beds. Even so, being out of doors at night was always frightening. You imagined enemy planes out there in the darkness of the Channel, coming ever closer.

But now Josie had another fear. Tomorrow was Monday. She would be going to the Mary Burnet School near Sloane Square. At the thought of entering a room full of strangers she felt butterflies in her stomach.

Chapter Three

An Unfriendly Girl

"This is Josephine Bishop."

Josie, standing beside Miss Hallam, was conscious that the entire class was assessing her. She pushed nervously at her glasses and tried not to catch anyone's eye.

"Josephine is Edith's cousin. She will be sharing our lessons for a few weeks while her mother is away. I know you will all do your best to make her feel welcome."

Welcome. That was what Josie wanted to feel, more than anything. She was determined to fit in, to be accepted.

"Josephine, there is a seat there, look, next to Alice."

It was a relief to sit down, away from the gaze of so many eyes. Josie sank gratefully into her place while Miss Hallam asked if the others had done their homework and then began talking about the war news.

"I hope you all listen to the radio at home? You know our shipping losses are high, and that means we must all make an effort not to waste anything. But we have had some successes, haven't we? Who can tell me where Harar and Keren are?"

Josie waited until a lot of other hands were up before raising hers.

"Iris?"

"East Africa, Miss Hallam."

"Correct. And some of your fathers may be serving

in Africa. Now, this might be a little more difficult. Who can point out Yugoslavia on the map?"

Josie only knew that Yugoslavia was somewhere in Europe. But Alice, the girl next to her, put her hand up at once. Everyone swiveled in their seats and watched as she went to the large map which filled the back wall of the room, and pointed it out.

"Thank you, Alice. Well done." (Josie saw Edith wrinkle her nose as she turned around to face front again.) "Yugoslavia is in the Balkans, isn't it? Who can tell me what happened in Yugoslavia recently...?"

Josie had no intention of answering questions on her first day. She slid a glance at Alice. Wasn't Alice the girl Edith had said was peculiar? It was certainly not normal to be able to find Yugoslavia on the world map. But she would have known this was the girl even if she hadn't done that. Alice was tall, with a droopy posture. Despite wearing a school uniform the same as everyone else's, she managed to look old-fashioned. Josie decided it must be her hair: instead of the usual bob she wore her light brown hair in a long single braid hanging down her back, untidily fastened with navy ribbon.

Edith sat across the way from Josie. She caught her eye and smiled when Miss Hallam's back was turned.

Miss Hallam, having finished the impromptu geography lesson, gave Josie an exercise book and a pen.

Their first lesson was reading comprehension. They were to read a short passage and answer questions on it. The textbooks were in their desks – or rather in some of them. Because books were in short supply they had to share. Alice moved her copy – unwillingly, Josie thought – toward the center of their pair of desks. She did not look at Josie, not even a quick glance.

She's unfriendly, Josie thought. Not welcoming at all.

After the brief flurry of desk opening and shutting, a deep hush descended, broken only by the scratching of Miss Hallam's pen and the tick of the clock on the wall behind her. The passage was from Hawthorne's book of Greek legends, and Josie had read it before. She found the questions easy. As she wrote down the answers she saw Alice writing equally fast.

Alice finished, put down her pen, and sat waiting. Josie had finished too, but she kept hold of her pen as if about to write some more, and glanced around the room.

The school might have been bombed, but this classroom was undamaged. It had tall church-like windows, too high to see out of, and a dais at one end where Miss Hallam sat at her desk in front of the blackboard. At the sides a number of empty desks had been pushed together. Josie counted those in use: eight pairs – sixteen girls, including herself. Some were quite young – ten or so; a few, including Alice, were about twelve.

As she looked around, Josie encountered other eyes – quick glances, most of them friendly, some merely curious. She saw that her cousin was a fidgety, mischievous girl, constantly whispering, turning around, signaling furtively across the room to a blonde girl who must be one of her friends. Once Miss Hallam looked up sharply and Edith subsided, head down over her work, but Josie caught her dimpled smile across the aisle. Aunty Grace would be shocked, she thought; but there had always been a lot that Aunty Grace didn't know about.

"Josephine," said Miss Hallam, startling her, "if you have finished you may collect the exercise books."

"Yes, Miss Hallam."

Josie stood up. Alice closed her exercise book and handed it to her. Josie felt embarrassed going around the room collecting books from strangers, but she took the opportunity to glance at the names on the covers. The blonde girl was Pamela Denham; the girl next to Edith, Clare Barrington. A skinny girl with buck teeth who grinned cheerfully at Josie was Sylvia Wells.

Before break they had a round of mental arithmetic.

Josie, who was not quick at math, kept her head low, but again Alice did well.

As they moved out of the classroom, Miss Hallam said, "Edith, show your cousin where the water fountain is; and the cloakroom."

"And the way to the air-raid shelter!" Sylvia was eager to show her everything.

Josie noticed that Alice had hung back, and was cleaning the blackboard for Miss Hallam.

The girls interrogated Josie as they all lined up at the water fountain on the playground.

"Where do you live?"

"Is there much bombing there?"

"Do you have any brothers or sisters?"

Josie told them everything except the truth about Ted. Without actually telling a lie she let them think he was in the RAF, like his cousin Peter. Edith caught her eye, and Josie gave her a look that said, "Don't tell. Please." She didn't think Edith would. They *were* cousins, after all; and Edith liked secrets.

Alice emerged just as they were all filing back in, and made for the drinking fountain.

"No time now, Alice! The bell's rung!" Pamela Denham called mockingly.

After the break Miss Hallam set them all some spelling words to learn. She wrote a list on the blackboard:

Incendiary

Artillery

Barrage

Conscription...

Then they all got out their knitting while Miss Hallam read to them from *Anne of Green Gables*. The knitting was socks, balaclavas or scarves for the Forces, depending on the knitter's degree of skill. Josie was given needles and khaki wool from a box in Miss Hallam's cabinet. With the teacher's promise of help, she embarked on a balaclava.

Several girls, among them Alice, Pamela and Sylvia, were expertly knitting socks on four needles. Edith was making rather a bad job of a scarf in Air Force blue. "Pity Peter if he gets this!" she whispered to Josie during one of *Anne*'s duller moments.

At twelve o'clock the entire school assembled in the hall for lunch. Here, there were signs of the bomb damage: a place where the roof had been hastily repaired, and dark water stains on one wall.

The oldest girls, from fourteen up, had come for dinner and would stay for afternoon lessons, while the younger ones went home.

"But not to idle away your time," Miss Hallam reminded them. "Remember that you have spelling to learn and an essay to write on how we can best help the war effort. Josephine, if you come and see me after dinner I'll give you the exact title for the essay."

By the time Josie had done this, and had also been asked by Miss Hallam how she was settling in, and about her grandmother's health, the others had gone: all except

Edith, who was waiting outside the classroom door.

They set off, and Josie said, "She's nice – Miss Hallam. And the girls."

"Shame you had to sit next to Alice."

"Not very friendly, is she?"

Edith rolled her eyes. "She never says a *word*."

Back home, they took off their school uniforms and changed into old clothes.

Edith's mother was not there.

"She's at work," said Edith. "Well, voluntary work. She's in the WVS. Most days she's out. They run a rescue center over at World's End. There's a canteen and they collect secondhand clothes and things, and do first aid. She'll be home by four." She smiled. "Which gives us about an hour and a half."

"For what? Our homework?"

Edith looked at her pityingly. She picked up her coat and headed for the back door. "Come on," she said.

Chapter Four

Bomb Site

They went up Flood Street and turned right onto the King's Road. A little way along Edith stopped and said, "We cross here."

Opposite, Josie saw a big furniture store with a long Tudor facade.

"That's where Alice Hampton lives," said Edith.

"That shop?"

Josie looked up, and saw the name, in gold lettering,

Hampton's, Established 1898; and underneath, *Fine Furniture, Clocks, Pianos*.

Above the shop were two more stories, and then gabled attics, the windows all screened with the regulation brown tape and blackout curtains.

They crossed over. Up-close, the furniture on display did not look as fine as the gold lettering promised. True, there were still some polished dark wooden tables and chairs, wardrobes and gilt-edged mirrors toward the back; but at the front was simpler stuff, some of it cut price, marked down as "Damaged by enemy action."

"Everyone who's bombed-out comes here," said Edith. "If they've still got any money, that is."

They walked on, then turned off into a side street. Another right turn, and they came upon a huge bomb site: a whole row of houses had been half demolished; only their lower stories were left. Heaps of brick rubble lay all around, and in the center was a vast crater full of debris.

"That used to be an apartment building," said Edith. "A landmine hit it. Loads of people were killed or injured."

The devastation was not recent; already weeds were growing there. The place had become a playground, and children were swarming over it. It must be out of bounds, Josie realized, but there was no warden to be seen. A gang of small boys was staging a battle, clambering across the piles of broken bricks, aiming stick guns. One wheeled past the girls with arms spread wide, being a plane. Their voices rang shrill. Farther off, some older boys seemed to be demolishing a shed.

Edith began scrambling over the rubble, and Josie followed. She saw that a group of girls had gathered in a makeshift shelter in the ruins. One of them waved: it was Edith's friend, Clare Barrington.

Edith and Josie made their way toward the group. Pam Denham was there too, and Sylvia Wells. They all looked quite different out of school uniform: less conspicuous, less likely to be well behaved.

However, all they were doing at that moment was squatting in a den built around the remains of someone's garden wall. Sylvia had discovered an old kettle and was encouraging the others to help her build a fireplace. "See: if we make a ring of bricks, here, and get some bits of wood, we can have a real fire!"

Sylvia and Clare began building the fireplace, while Josie went with Edith to look for wood. Their search took them near the group of older boys. One of them called out, "Hey, Edith! Who's your friend?"

Edith turned to him with her dimpled smile. "Josie," she said. "She's my cousin."

"Hallo, Josie!"

He grinned at her: tall, fair-haired, scruffy-looking, but self-assured. A show-off, Josie thought. All the same, it was flattering to have been noticed.

"That's Vic," said Edith, as they moved on.

"Does he live around here?" She could see that Vic was not the sort of boy Aunty Grace would approve of.

Or her own mother, for that matter.

"I think so," said Edith. "His dad has a grocery store."

Josie noticed that Edith had subtly altered her accent and way of speaking to sound more like Vic's.

There were bits of window frame everywhere, some with shards of glass still attached. They avoided those, and carefully broke a few of the others into manageable pieces and brought them back to lay in the fireplace.

They were all absorbed in this task when a voice spoke behind them. "Playing housey, girls?"

"Clear off, Vic," said Pam, surprising Josie with a turn of phrase that Miss Hallam would certainly not expect to hear her use.

"Unless you've got matches," said Sylvia.

Of course he had. A boy like Vic would always have matches. He kneeled down next to Josie and lit one, cupping his hand around the flame. But the wood was damp and refused to light. The splintered ends caught, flared briefly, blackened and went out.

"Useless," said Vic. The remark seemed to encompass the whole arrangement, the girls, the game itself. "We're breaking up that shed. You'll see a real fire later on."

But no sign of it appeared. The boys continued their wrecking, and the girls grew bored with the den and played tag, and then switched to stalking games which involved hanging around near the boys, running and squealing.

Suddenly Josie saw a familiar figure walking along a footpath at the edge of the bomb site.

"There's Alice Hampton!" she said.

Alice still wore her navy blue school coat and carried her bookbag.

"She'll be off to her lessons," said Edith. "She has private tutoring twice a week, so that she doesn't get behind because of the war. I heard her telling Miss Hallam."

"Private tutoring!" Sylvia's voice rose to a squawk. "She needs to be *less* brainy, that one!"

"Where's she going, then?" asked Pam.

They took off across the bomb site in pursuit. Josie followed, feeling uneasy, wishing she had not mentioned seeing the girl.

"Hey! Alice! Brainbox!"

They stopped and surrounded her.

"Where are you going, Brainbox?"

Alice's eyes darted from one to another of them. "Leave me alone."

"We just want to know where you're going," said Pam. Her words were reasonable enough, but she was a hefty girl; intimidating.

"Have you come to play with *us*?" asked Sylvia, giggling at the idea.

"I'm going to a class. I'll be late." Alice started forward, but they kept alongside her. She began to run, her bookbag bouncing on her back, her braid tossing from side to side.

They let her go, and drifted back to the bomb site.

"What's the time?" asked Clare.

No one had a watch. They ran into the street where a church clock said a quarter past three.

"We'd better get home," said Edith.

The group split up, to Josie's relief. She'd enjoyed the games, but not the baiting of Alice Hampton; that reminded her too much of the way she'd been picked on at her own school in Greenwich.

She and Edith hurried home and hung up their coats.

"Quick," said Edith. "The books."

She opened her bookbag and took out books, a pencil, an eraser and laid them on the dining table. Josie did the same. Twenty minutes later, when her aunt came in, they were both doing their homework.

"Hallo, girls!" she said, putting her head around the door. "Busy? I see Miss Hallam has given you homework already, Josie!"

Josie blushed and looked down at her work. She felt ashamed at deceiving her aunt like this.

A few minutes later they heard Aunt Grace's voice

from the far end of the hall, at the back door. "Oh, Biddy! Poor thing! Didn't Edith let you in? Hasn't she fed you?"

"Drat," said Edith softly.

Her mother appeared in the doorway with the neglected cat in noisy attendance.

"Has Biddy been outside all this time?" she asked. "You don't seem to have fed her."

"I forgot," said Edith. "We were talking – and things. She can't have meowed much."

"She was meowing when *I* came in, poor thing," said Aunty Grace.

Biddy had the offended air of a cat who has meowed long and hard and been ignored. Now she kept close to Aunty Grace, following her eagerly as she went into the kitchen.

Edith grinned, and said in a low voice, "Remind me about Biddy next time."

She clearly had no remorse, but Josie felt bad about the cat, about the deceit, about everything. When it began to get dark, she got up and offered to draw the blackout curtains around the apartment.

"Oh, that would be a help, Josie," said her aunt. "The bathroom one is a bit awkward; it's a board that has to be hung on pegs. Edith will show you. I must get on with the dinner..."

She made shepherd's pie for dinner, but there was hardly any meat in it. Josie didn't like the mixture of turnips, carrots and beans, and Edith made a face when her mother wasn't looking; but they all ate it – they were too hungry to be fussy.

Aunty Grace made a pot of tea – weak, to save the ration. As they cleared away the dishes she said, "Shall we have some music? Have a look at the gramophone records, Josie, and choose something you like."

But at that moment an unearthly sound penetrated the house: the rising wail of the air-raid siren.

Chapter Five

Air Raid

“Bother!” said Aunty Grace. It was a strong word for her.

If she felt fear she didn’t show it. “Go down, girls. I’ll follow with the tea.” She began pouring the three cups of tea into a thermos flask.

Josie wanted to run. She always felt panic when she heard that sinister rising and falling wail. At home it meant a dash to the back door, where her mother kept a bag of nightclothes and other essentials ready packed, and then out into the cold dark garden.

But here there was no Anderson shelter.

"Down these steps." Edith had seized Biddy before the startled cat could protest, and now she opened a door in the hall and switched on a flashlight. In the pale circle of light Josie saw steps curving down, and at the same time she heard the throb of approaching bombers. Edith went first with the cat, and Josie followed, turning right at the bottom into a large room full of shadowy objects.

Behind her came her aunt with the thermos of tea and what looked like a cookie tin. When they were all assembled, Aunty Grace lit a paraffin lamp; and as the strong bright light intensified Josie was able to see around. The room was furnished with a folding table and chairs, and three camp beds made up with blankets and pillows. There was an old kitchen cupboard with the doors open, full of books and games. There were shelves of food: dried milk, orange juice, cans of baked beans, Spam and corned beef. And a basket of knitting, buckets of sand and water, a toolbox, a first-aid kit, candle holders, towels, a bowl to wash in… Aunty Grace was very thorough, Josie thought. She'd seen such rooms illustrated in her mother's magazines, but Mummy had said no one would really *do* all those things.

She felt safer now. People said a cellar wasn't as safe as an Anderson, that you could be buried alive if the house collapsed, but it *felt* strong. And she knew there were sandbags all around the walls and the doors were reinforced. Best of all, it looked comfortable.

"It's like a whole separate house!" she said. "Our Anderson is horrible – all spidery and damp, and nowhere to move."

"There's another room too," said Edith. She showed Josie. "This used to be the laundry in the olden days, when they had servants."

She shone the flashlight around and showed Josie a room full of junk: old bicycles, a baby carriage, a decayed wicker chair, flowerpots. There was also a shallow stone sink and a fireplace and a big old tub that Edith said was once used for washing clothes.

"Switch that flashlight off, Edith," her mother said. "Come and drink your tea."

They sat down, and to Josie's delight Biddy jumped onto her lap. She stroked the cat. "Don't worry, Biddy. Hitler can't get you here."

As if to prove her wrong, there came the thud of a distant bomb, followed by a series of loud bangs that caused Biddy to leap off Josie's lap and vanish under a bed.

They heard voices close by. Josie looked up, startled.

"That's the upstairs tenants," her aunt said. She nodded toward a closed door on the other side of the stairs. "We've agreed to share the basement for the duration. They come down the outside steps into their half."

She stood up as someone knocked on the connecting

door and a woman's voice called, "Are you there, Mrs. Felgate?"

Josie's aunt opened the door. A woman came in: tall, with neatly rolled fair hair and a look of natural authority about her. She wore an air-raid warden's uniform and was holding her tin hat.

"Everything under control?" she asked. "No problems? Cat safe?"

"We're quite all right, Miss Rutherford, thank you. I didn't think you were on duty tonight?"

"I'm not, officially, but I phoned HQ to ask if they could do with any help. Seems Bertie Melford's away, so I said I'd go in. I'm just off to do a check of the street." Her glance took in Josie. "This must be your niece?"

"Yes, this is Josie – Josephine Bishop."

Miss Rutherford shook Josie's hand; she had a firm grip. "Pleased to meet you. Nice for Edith to have company."

She put on her tin hat and went back through the doorway.

Then the other people came in: an elderly couple, the old man walking with the aid of a stick. There were more introductions.

"You remember Mr. and Mrs. Prescott, don't you, Josie?"

Embarrassed by all this adult attention, Josie looked around for Edith, but her cousin was half under a bed, trying to persuade Biddy to come out.

The Prescotts and Felgates were evidently in the habit of spending air raids together. Mrs. Prescott fetched her knitting and a thermos and the two women settled down to talk while Mr. Prescott read a newspaper.

Mrs. Prescott turned to Josie. "I seem to recall that you had an elder brother, Josie?"

Josie took a breath. "Yes," she said – and braced herself.

But before she could be asked any more, Edith erupted from under the bed. She grabbed at the cat, which leaped out of her arms, landed on the table, and skidded off, knocking over a cup of tea before disappearing under another bed.

Both girls collapsed in giggles. Mrs. Prescott dabbed at the spilled tea with a handkerchief, while Edith, still laughing, tried to entice the cat out again.

"Edith!" her mother remonstrated. "Leave Biddy where she is."

"That cat doesn't like me," said Edith.

"I'm not surprised. You only bother with her when she doesn't want you – and you forget to feed her. Why don't you and Josie find a quiet game to play?"

Yes, thought Josie. Something that will keep us away from the grownups. Aunty Grace obviously hadn't told her neighbors about Ted, but now, when they could all be here together for several hours, the two women would be sure to talk about their families. Mrs. Prescott might ask about Ted, and Josie knew that Aunty Grace would not tell a lie.

But at first, as Edith rummaged among the games, the adults talked about Miss Rutherford.

"I do admire her," said Josie's aunt. "She works so hard. She's in that office in Whitehall all day; then she takes on the warden's post in the evening."

"She's a very committed person," agreed Mrs. Prescott.

The whistle of a descending bomb sounded overhead and Aunty Grace looked up sharply and exclaimed, "Edith! Girls! Come here!"

They all huddled close together as the crash came, somewhere nearby. Josie felt the walls shaking. Perhaps the whole house was shaking. It was an old house. She imagined the ancient timbers giving way, the floors falling through, the way she'd seen them sometimes in other houses after a night's bombing: buildings collapsed in on themselves, reduced to a pile of wood and bricks. I wish Mummy was here, she thought; then I wouldn't have to pretend I'm not scared.

"It's not as near as it sounds," said Aunty Grace.

Mr. Prescott agreed. "Belgravia, I'd say."

"Battersea caught it last night," said his wife.

"Miss Rutherford was telling us."

They heard the guns start up.

"Those are ours."

They had all become expert at interpreting the sounds. When you could put a name to what was happening, Josie thought, you didn't feel quite so defenseless.

The guns went quiet again, and Edith drew Josie away and showed her the packs of cards and puzzle books in the cupboard. They played *Blackout!* and *Old Maid*, and then *Snap*.

As they slapped down the cards Josie half listened to the adults' conversation. Don't mention Ted, she silently begged her aunt. Don't let all that trouble follow me here.

"*Snap!*" Edith grinned at her. "You weren't paying attention!"

Chapter Six

Bad Company

The next day Edith and Josie went off early to school, eager to find signs of the previous night's bombing and to look for shrapnel. There was nothing nearby, but when they reached Pimlico Road they saw that a bomb had fallen on Elm Walk. The pavement was the usual mess of broken glass and brick debris, and the smell of cordite hung in the air. People were sweeping the paths and pavement as if the glass were autumn leaves.

Josie spotted the tailfin of an incendiary bomb and picked it up.

"Oh! That's good!" Edith scuffed around with her shoe, hoping for another souvenir. There were some bits of metal, but they were too large and jagged to take to school. "They'll be gone by the time we get back," she said.

An air-raid warden came and shooed them away. "You girls should be at school!"

Reluctantly they left and walked to Norton Terrace and into school. The girls there were all in a state of excitement about last night's raid. One of them came from Elm Walk; and there had been another bomb in Belgravia, where some of the others lived. There were stories of windows blown in, dogs gone missing, incendiaries put out with a stirrup pump, shrapnel found the next morning. Before Christmas the bombers had come every night, but this was the first raid for a week or so and everyone was talking about it.

They filed into the hall for Assembly. Miss Gregory,

the headmistress, led the prayers. She told the girls to think of their fathers, uncles and brothers serving abroad, all of them risking their lives to protect Britain from invasion.

Edith leaned toward Josie. "All except Ted," she whispered.

"Shut up!"

So much for Edith saying she doesn't blame *me*, Josie thought; she still can't resist a dig.

"We shall sing hymn number 261," said Miss Gregory. "'Bless'd are the pure in heart.'"

As they began singing Edith whispered again, "I didn't mean it."

No; but you said it, Josie thought.

She sang:

"The LORD, Who left the heavens

Our life and peace to bring,

To dwell in lowliness with men,

Their Pattern and their King..."

Ted had said to her, the day he went to his tribunal,

"It'd be easier if I was religious – a member of some church, or a Quaker. They think no one else has a conscience. I'll need to convince them that I truly believe we should not go to war; that I'm just not prepared to be part of it."

"*...Still to the lowly soul*

He doth Himself impart..."

When Assembly was over and they went into the classroom, Josie took her seat next to Alice Hampton. She didn't want to sit next to Alice now; she felt guilty and embarrassed. But if Alice resented her, she didn't show it; neither was she any more friendly. Josie wanted to say, "It wasn't me – wasn't my idea," but Alice gave her no way to make amends.

During the morning it began to rain, and by lunchtime it was far too wet and cold to go to the bomb site. Edith and Josie hurried home. Edith's mother had left a shopping list for them, so they went to Oakley Street and bought groceries: dried milk, a tiny amount of butter and cheese, bacon, sugar, bread;

and their own candy ration: Josie chose aniseed balls and Edith had sherbet lemons. "Then we can share," she said.

Josie enjoyed shopping in a place where she was not known. At home in Greenwich the shopkeepers were often cool toward her, and she would sometimes be aware of curious or hostile glances from other customers. Once, she had walked into Hollamby's when the shop was crowded and full of the buzz of conversation, only for the place to fall silent at her appearance.

Aunty Grace came home and put the shopping away, shaking her head over the small size of the butter ration. She began cooking while the girls did their homework.

That night there was no bombing.

"Too cloudy," said Aunty Grace. She was relieved, and sat knitting and listening to the radio while Josie wrote a letter to her mother and Edith teased the cat.

The next afternoon – Wednesday – Edith said, "I've got Red Cross Cadets group at two, at the church hall. We're learning first aid. Do you want to come?"

"If they'll let me."

They did; and the two of them spent the afternoon with a group of cadets and two women from the Red Cross, bandaging, splinting and resuscitating each other.

It was Thursday before they went to the bomb site again. This time the boys had the promised fire alight, fed with wood from the smashed-up shed. The girls stood around watching.

The usual boys were there: Vic; his younger brother Stan; and Ray, a big, excitable boy of about thirteen.

"You'll get the warden after you, lighting that fire," said Clare.

Stan laughed. "We're not scared of him!"

Edith turned to Vic. He was the one whose attention the girls all vied for. "Did you get any shrapnel on Tuesday? We found a bit of an incendiary."

"*I* found it," said Josie. She brought it out of her pocket to show him.

But Vic was unimpressed. "I've got tons of those. Got a bit off a Dornier –"

"I've got a dial –"

"We found an unexploded bomb –"

A clamor of voices, male and female, had broken out. Ray waved his arms about, telling a story about a grenade he'd picked up and taken home. "Threw it in the backyard – whoosh! – bits of fence everywhere! Dad went crazy!"

Vic drew Edith and Josie aside. "Have a look at this."

Out of his pocket he brought a watch. Josie sensed instantly that it was stolen. It was a man's watch, gold, expensive-looking, with a brown leather strap, and had a tiny second hand that went around in its own circle.

Edith drew in her breath. "Where did you get that? You stole it, didn't you?"

"Found it," said Vic. "Found a few things, me and Stan."

Stan had joined them. "Those houses in Belmont Walk," he said, "they're all empty. Chace Terrace as well, and Ruyter Street. Rows of society houses, no one living there, all their furniture and stuff left behind. The owners have skipped out."

"Gone to their country homes for the duration," said Vic. "Jewelery and all sorts left lying around..."

"You broke in?" Edith sounded shocked, but Josie could see that she was impressed.

"It's easy. The cellars are the best way. And those people don't need the stuff, or they'd have taken it with them."

"But – it's still stealing," said Josie.

Vic shrugged. "Rescue services do it all the time, don't they? Our cousin's a fireman. Says it's one of the perks. Anything small, like that. Or stuff you can sell."

Josie didn't want to believe him. But Clare, who'd been listening, said, "It's true. My aunty's house in

Hampstead was looted after she was bombed out. She says it must have been the rescue workers."

Josie didn't like to think of that: men risking their own lives to save others, but robbing them at the same time. Did that make them heroes, or villains?

"There's your loopy friend," said Vic, glancing across the waste ground.

Josie saw Alice Hampton hurrying along the road, head down.

"She's not our friend!" retorted Edith.

And Sylvia said, "She's a drip."

They left the boys, and Josie hoped they would choose a game – skipping, or tag. But it seemed the game was to be taunting Alice. They began to pick up small pieces of brick debris and flick them, as if accidentally, in her direction, all the time drawing closer. Then, with Pam in the lead, they set off in pursuit.

Josie hung back. But Edith said, "Come *on*!" – and she went along with them, afraid to be singled out, shown up as different.

They surrounded Alice; blocked her way. She tried to push past them, but Pam and Edith dodged from side to side, laughing, outwitting her, keeping her trapped. "Don't run away! We're coming with you to your class. Then we can all learn to be teacher's pets."

Alice ignored them. Sylvia sneaked up behind her and pulled her braid, untying the ribbon, which slipped out. Clare tugged at her bag. "Let's have a look at your books! What are you learning? Let's see."

"Leave me *alone*!" Alice shouted.

Josie appealed to her cousin. "Edith, let her go. It's mean."

But Edith wasn't listening. She was full of the excitement of the chase. Alice broke free of them, but they ran after her and caught up. Josie followed, unwillingly.

They only fell back when Alice turned the corner into Belmont Gardens, and they saw that she was heading for one of the houses there.

"So that's where she goes," said Pam.

The group split up, and Edith and Josie set off home down the King's Road.

Josie walked ahead, knowing her feelings must be obvious to her cousin.

"It's just a game," said Edith. "We're not hurting her."

"It's mean."

"So what? No one likes her. *You* don't like her, do you?"

"No."

"Well, it doesn't matter, then, does it?"

But Josie felt that it did.

The next day, at school, she said to Alice, "I tried to stop them from chasing you."

But Alice only shrugged and said, "You needn't bother. I don't care."

At break times Alice stayed in, doing tasks for Miss Hallam: filling inkwells, or tidying the stationery cupboard.

"She's a teacher's pet," said Sylvia.

Or she's scared to come out because of us, thought Josie. But she didn't say so.

On Friday they followed Alice home from school after lunch. They walked at a discreet distance – mindful of the fact that they were in school uniform – but they spoke loudly about creeps and teacher's pets. Josie knew Alice must be all too aware of them. When she reached her family's shop she opened a side door and glanced back with a hunted expression before going in and closing the door behind her.

I ought to stick up for her, Josie thought, whether she wants me to or not. But Josie had been the victim herself at school in Greenwich. It wouldn't take much for Edith's friends to turn against her. She pushed at her glasses – a nervous movement. If she didn't seem to be their sort; if she wouldn't go along with them; if Edith let slip a hint about Ted (and she might; you couldn't trust Edith)... Why should she risk it, sticking up for a girl no one liked?

"Josie! Come on!" called Sylvia. "We're going over to Lennox Square. Vic says there's lots of shrapnel…"

They like me, she thought. I'm part of the group. It was a good feeling. She desperately wanted it to last.

Chapter Seven

Trouble

On Monday morning, before prayers began, Miss Gregory said, "I should like to see the following girls in my office after Assembly: Clare Barrington; Pamela Denham; Sylvia Wells; Edith Felgate; and Josephine Bishop."

A murmur was heard throughout the hall. Everyone knew that being called to see Miss Gregory meant trouble. Josie felt a sinking sensation in her stomach;

her hands turned clammy. She'd only been here a week and already she was up before the headmistress. It must be about Alice Hampton, she thought. In desperation she looked at Edith, but her cousin only shrugged and widened her eyes as if she couldn't imagine why they had been summoned.

After that, the prayers and hymns washed over Josie, unheeded; she could take in nothing except the fact that she had to go and see Miss Gregory.

When the hall began to empty, the five of them drew together and made their way to Miss Gregory's office. Josie had never felt less happy about being part of the group. Clare's face was set hard. "That Alice has told on us! She's gone sneaking to Miss Hallam!"

"She'll be sorry if she has," said Pam.

They stood outside the door, whispering. Edith said, "Do you think she'll see us one by one?" and Sylvia whimpered at the thought.

Then Miss Gregory opened her door, and they all fell silent.

"Come in, girls," she said.

Of the two teachers, Miss Gregory was the one everyone was afraid of. From what Josie had heard, she was a formidable woman with no time for excuses. One glance from her had been known to reduce a girl to tears. Sylvia was sniffling already.

Josie was too frightened to cry; she kept her head low, and so did Clare. Pam was wearing her belligerent "it wasn't me" look; and Edith, gazing wide-eyed at Miss Gregory, appeared so innocent and well-brought-up that it was difficult to imagine her being accused of anything.

"Sylvia, use your handkerchief," said Miss Gregory with distaste.

Her gaze swept over all five of them.

"I have heard reports that you girls have been seen playing with boys on a bomb site near Belmont Gardens. Is this true?"

So that was it. No mention of bullying Alice – unless she was leading up to that, Josie thought.

"Yes, Miss Gregory" – a murmured chorus.

Miss Gregory assumed an air of feigned weariness. "Day after day," she said, "I have stressed the dangers of playing on bomb sites: danger from falls, from cuts, from unstable buildings, even from unexploded bombs. Most of your mothers are at work or helping the war effort in some way. They can't be watching over you all the time. They rely on you, as I do, as your country does, to behave in a sensible manner. Do you think you have behaved responsibly, and set a good example to the younger girls?"

"No, Miss Gregory."

"No, indeed. But there is another, even more important aspect to this. Girls, I think you know the school's motto: 'Hold fast that which is good.' That means your behavior in and out of school should be beyond reproach. We try, even in these difficult wartime circumstances, to encourage you to become good citizens. We hope each of you will take the values you learn in school out into the community, that each of you will be a credit to the school. Playing on bomb sites, with *boys*" – she said the word as if boys were an alien form of life, Josie thought – "is hardly the way for young ladies to behave, is it?"

"No, Miss Gregory," they chorused dutifully.

"I am ashamed of you," continued the headmistress, her voice growing rich with indignation. "Now, at a time when civilization is at risk and standards more important than ever before, you have let down the school and cast a slur on everyone here. I am surprised at *you*, Edith" – Edith looked up, startled, outraged at being singled out – "leading your cousin astray in her first week with us."

Josie felt impelled to say, "Edith didn't—" but Miss Gregory silenced her with a look.

"I hope that I shall not have to speak to you again about this. If any further lapses occur I will be obliged to inform your parents. Meanwhile, I expect you to go straight home after school."

Edith fixed the teacher with her wide blue gaze.

"But, Miss Gregory, we do! We weren't on the bomb site in uniform."

"Edith, a Mary Burnet girl behaves like a lady at all times – is that clear? – not merely when she is in uniform. The school's reputation is in your hands."

"Yes, Miss Gregory."

"You will all be given extra homework and you will go straight home and stay there."

"Yes, Miss Gregory."

Outside, Pam exploded. "It's not *fair*! *Everyone* goes on bomb sites! Why pick on us? And who told her?"

"It's Alice," said Clare. "She's getting back at us. She's ratted."

Josie found that hard to believe. No one went running to teachers, no matter what happened.

Sylvia agreed. "It was probably a neighbor – some nosy old bag."

"An old bag who knew all our names?"

That made it suspicious.

"We'll get her this for this," said Pam.

In the classroom, a lesson was already in progress, and all eyes were on the five girls as they went to their seats. Afterwards Miss Hallam delivered a warning to the whole class about the dangers of playing on bomb sites and collecting shrapnel. She didn't mention any names, but everyone must have known what had happened. Alice kept her head down over her work, and Josie wondered if she really had told Miss Gregory. But even if she hadn't, someone – perhaps the tutor in Belmont Gardens – must have got the names from Alice.

There was no opportunity for revenge while they were at school. Alice stayed behind when they went out at break; and after lunch, when everyone was going home, she was nowhere to be seen.

They waited for her round the corner, pretending to look in shop windows. Josie felt anxious and had no wish to confront Alice.

"Let's go home," she whispered to her cousin.

"Edith, Miss Gregory said we should go straight home."

"Go on, then, if you're scared. I'm staying."

"But –"

"Here she comes!"

Alice saw them and tried to cross the road, but they surrounded her – like a pack of wolves, thought Josie unhappily.

And yet the girl deserved it. You could see the guilt in her face.

"You told on us!"

"You sneaked to Miss Gregory!"

They pushed and jostled her as she tried to get away.

"Admit it! It was you, wasn't it?"

"Let me go!" said Alice.

"Why did you report us?"

"I didn't."

"You did!"

"I didn't tell Miss Gregory."

"You told someone."

"You're a creep."

With each accusation Pam and Clare gave her a push.

Some shoppers came by – two women with a child and a baby in a carriage – and they were obliged to ease off. Alice seized the opportunity to move away. With a surprising flash of defiance she turned back and flung at them, "If you don't want to be reported you shouldn't go there!"

This caused the women to look up in surprise and disapproval. Alice ran off, and the rest of them could not pursue her without squeezing past the carriage and drawing more attention to themselves.

"I'm off home now," said Pam.

"Me, too."

"And me."

"Mind you don't meet any boys," joked Edith.

"Boys!" exclaimed Clare. "Ugh! How dreadful!"

"A Mary Burnet girl does not associate with *boys*!"

said Pam. "She holds fast that which is good."

They all struck holding-fast attitudes.

"Civilization!"

"Standards!"

"Responsibility!"

Then, with "Bye! See you tomorrow," they split up, Clare and Sylvia following in the direction Alice had gone, Pam heading for Sloane Square, Edith and Josie for the Embankment.

It was understood, without saying, that they would not meet up at the bomb site today.

When Edith and Josie reached home there were some letters lying on the mat.

"There's one for you," said Edith.

"Oh! From Mummy!"

Josie opened it carefully so that the envelope could be reused.

Edith hovered, peering to see.

"Go away!"

Biddy could be heard, meowing outside the back

door. Edith went to let her in, and Josie escaped to the hiding place at the top of the stairs.

Granny was doing well, her mother said, but it would still be several weeks before she could be left on her own. They'd had some bombing last week; did Chelsea have it too? She hoped Josie was being a good girl (Josie bit her lip as she read that) and no trouble to Aunty Grace. And that she was wearing her vest and remembering to take her Virol and cod-liver oil.

"Now here's some good news," her mother continued. "Ted has some leave in about ten days' time. He says he'll stay in Greenwich (he'll be able to check on Russ) but come and visit us here in Dagenham; and he plans to visit you, too..."

Ted! Coming here! Josie's heart leaped in delight and alarm. Ted had had no leave since before Christmas, and she longed to see him. But at the same time she felt panic-stricken. Suppose someone saw her with him – someone from school? Suppose someone asked what he did? Or Edith let something slip? Edith would be bursting; she'd be sure to drop hints. If only he didn't have to come *here*, Josie thought. And then she felt ashamed: how *could* she think she didn't want her brother to come and see her?

"Josie? Are you up there?"

Josie folded the letter and put it in her pocket. She'd have to tell Edith about Ted coming – but not yet.

Chapter Eight

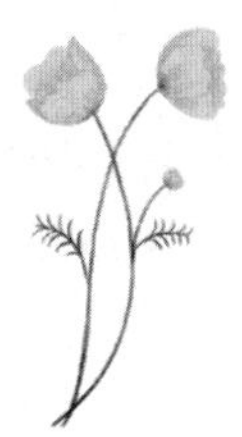

The Top-Floor Apartment

The girls continued their persecution of Alice Hampton the next day. At school they had to be careful – there were teachers about and Alice took care to stay in at break. But she couldn't escape them entirely. They hissed "Sneak!" and "Creep!" at her in passing. Pam and Edith caught her in the toilets and held her cubicle door shut so that she couldn't get out, while Clare, in the next cubicle, flung a cup of water over her from the top of the partition.

"We told her it was water from the toilet," Edith told Josie.

"But it wasn't?"

"Ugh! No! We wouldn't touch that!"

Josie saw them catch her again at the end of break. Alice was hiding among the coats in the cloakroom, and they dragged her out, pinched her and pulled her hair – all before anyone had time to notice.

When school ended for the day they planned another ambush.

"Come on, Josie," Edith said – and Josie followed, reluctantly.

They lay in wait around a corner off Sloane Street, and this time Pam and Edith were armed with handfuls of gravel.

Josie wasn't happy. "Edith, I'm going home."

"You haven't got a key."

"I don't care. We'll get into trouble, doing this. And anyway, it's not fair."

"Not fair!" Pam was indignant. "After what she did to us?"

"We started it before that." Josie struggled to explain. "I don't like her either. But – even if she did tell on us, it's not right…all this. It just makes things worse."

The others stared. Pam rolled her eyes. Sylvia giggled and said, "Are you a Conchie or something?"

"What?" Josie felt as if she'd been punched – and at the same moment she heard Edith give a yelp of laughter. "No!" Josie said, too loudly. "Don't be stupid!"

Edith gave her a look that said "serves you right."

She'll tell, Josie thought. She'd tell without a thought if it suited her.

And then Sylvia hissed, "Here's Alice!" and their prey appeared. Clare and Sylvia jumped out and grabbed her while the other two stuffed gravel down the back of her coat and blouse.

In the scuffle that ensued, Josie hung back. She

wanted to go on ahead to Chelsea Walk; she was ashamed of herself for not going. But she feared what Edith might say to the others about her if she ran off.

Alice, who had never shown much emotion before, was almost in tears when they'd finished with her. She ran off toward the King's Road with small stones cascading around her, her hair escaping from the braid.

Edith turned her aggression on Josie as the two of them walked home. "You needn't think I'll break up with Pam and the others."

"I never asked you to. I just asked you to leave Alice alone." Josie knew it came to the same thing; that she was asking too much.

"They think you're wet, my friends."

My friends. I'm going to be shut out here, just as I was at home, thought Josie, if I don't go along with them. Even Edith will turn against me.

She was aware of the atmosphere between them as they walked on, together but apart. "Shall we get our candy?" she asked. "Go down to the Embankment?"

Edith agreed. They went to Melford's and chose candies to share, then dawdled by the river, sucking peppermints. They watched the boats going by and saw some women in ATS uniform tying down a barrage balloon, and soldiers guarding the guns by Battersea Bridge. Edith became friendlier now that she was away from her school friends, and by the time they had returned to the house they were chatting easily together in their usual way.

Aunty Grace came home and said, "Oh, Edith, you're not eating candy? You know you're going to the dentist this afternoon?"

"I forgot." Edith crunched her peppermint.

"You'd better give your teeth a good cleaning. Josie, you don't want to come, do you?" Josie shook her head; she hated the smell and atmosphere of dentists'. "We shouldn't be too late back, although I couldn't get an appointment before five-thirty. I'll put the dinner in a low oven..."

Josie rather liked being left alone in the house. She found the family's photograph album and looked at the pictures. She played with Biddy, and read a bit of *The Three Musketeers*, and finished her candies. Then she went into the garden and climbed the walnut tree. She sat on a high branch and looked out over the back-garden wall, across Flood Street. Somewhere out there, beyond those rooftops, was the Mary Burnet School. She thought again about being called to see the headmistress yesterday. She'd been so frightened and ashamed. She'd never been in that sort of trouble before; her mother would be horrified if she found out. And Alice Hampton... That was more trouble brewing. She wished the others would just leave the girl alone.

She heard the side gate creak, and looked down. Miss Rutherford came in, wearing a gray tweed suit and a little hat with a feather in it. She was carrying a shopping bag.

She glanced up and saw Josie.

"Hallo! On your own today?"

"Edith's gone to the dentist. Aunty Grace took her."

"Poor Edith!" Miss Rutherford took out her key and was about to go inside when she turned back and said, "Are you peckish? I've got some homemade jam – if you'd like to come up?"

Josie felt shy. But it seemed rude to refuse, and she *was* hungry; and it would be interesting, she thought, to see Miss Rutherford's apartment.

"Yes, please," she said, and scrambled down.

She followed Miss Rutherford up two flights of stairs. There was a telephone on the midway landing, and a bucket of sand and a stirrup pump; and more firefighting equipment at the bottom of the attic stairs.

"Have you been in the attic?" she asked shyly, peering up. She had a fascination with attics; she liked their sloping roofs and little low windows.

"Good heavens, yes!" said Miss Rutherford. "They're not locked, and all the clutter has been taken away. Had to be, under the Clearance of Lofts Act, in case of fire. We had incendiaries through the roof one night last year." She caught Josie's look of interest and said, "Run up and see, if you like. I'll unpack and put the kettle on."

Josie climbed up into the empty rooms, her footsteps echoing as she moved from the back to the front of the house. The back view from the small gable window was one of crowded rooftops, but from the front you could see right across the river and beyond.

She went downstairs and found Miss Rutherford in her small kitchen.

"I'd love to sleep up there!"

Miss Rutherford laughed. "I think of attics as a place for maidservants to sleep."

"Do you think maids *did* sleep there?"

"I know they did. I had a maid here myself before the last war."

Josie was surprised. "Have you lived here all that time?"

"No. But I used to live in this apartment when I was

younger. I rented it from a relative. Last year, when I was looking for an apartment in Chelsea, he told me it was empty again. So I came back."

She began cutting bread, and nodded toward the living room. "Make yourself at home. I'll bring things in. Luckily for you, I went shopping on my way home from work and bought some fresh bread."

Josie went into the living room, which was surprisingly large and comfortable. Somehow, when Edith had described Miss Rutherford as "spinster," she had imagined someone living a mean, cramped existence. But Miss Rutherford had expensive-looking furniture, a soft brown patterned carpet, paintings on the walls, and shelves of books.

Josie went to look at the books. There were poetry books, a few novels that looked rather long and dull, several books that seemed to be about politics...

"Nothing much to interest you, I'm afraid."

Miss Rutherford had come in with a tray of tea cups, milk and sugar, which she placed on a low table.

"I like your paintings," said Josie. "That one especially."

It was a picture of Miss Rutherford when she was much younger, but you could still see that it was her. She wore a pale green dress and there was a glass vase of roses on the table beside her. It was a summery picture that made Josie think of life before the war.

"A friend painted that," said Miss Rutherford.

Josie was impressed. "Someone famous?"

"He never had the chance to become famous. He was killed in the trenches in 1917, aged twenty-three."

Josie absorbed this information. She wanted to ask, "Did you love him?" but didn't dare.

Miss Rutherford had returned to the kitchen, and now she came back with tea, bread, a pot of jam and even a small dish of butter.

"My mother made the jam. It's excellent. Now, where do you want to sit?"

"May I sit on this?"

"This" was a long seat, like a sofa but more upright,

with a wooden padded back that curved around one end. It was upholstered in faded green velvet and had two green and gold cushions.

"Yes, of course! The chaise longue. I like that too."

"Chaise longue?"

"It means 'long chair.' You're supposed to lounge on it – though not when you're drinking tea! You put your feet up and lie along the length and read a book and eat chocolates."

"Chocolates!" said Josie blissfully. She had not seen any for a long time.

"Mmm… Those were the days, weren't they?" Miss Rutherford poured tea into delicate fluted cups. "I bought the chaise longue when I first moved here, in 1914. I fell in love with it. It was in Hauptmann's – that lovely furniture store in the King's Road, near The Pheasantry."

At the mention of the shop Josie's heart had begun to race. But – "Haupt – do you mean Hampton's?" she asked.

"Hampton's! Yes, of course. They changed their name after the last war."

"Changed their name? Why?"

"They were German. And Germans living in Britain suffered a good deal of harassment during the war. I believe the owner was even interned for a while as an enemy alien. Quite ridiculous. He'd lived here since his twenties."

"So" – Josie was staring at her – "it's the same family? They're really Germans?"

"Yes. But the present owner was born here, and has an English name. They're hardly foreigners now."

But Josie was thinking: Alice Hampton is German. Her name should really be Alice Hauptmann.

"It was such fun furnishing this place," said Miss Rutherford. "I shared it with a friend, another girl. And then the war began..."

"What did you do in the war?" It was hard to imagine that other war, long ago, and Miss Rutherford young in that green dress.

"I was a nurse," she said. "I worked in France." She sighed and shook her head. "And now we are in another war. I suppose your father is in the Services?"

"Yes. He's somewhere in North Africa – in the Army."

"You must miss him?"

"Yes." She paused. It was on the tip of her tongue to tell Miss Rutherford about Ted, all about him; somehow she felt her new acquaintance would not be shocked. But before she could speak Miss Rutherford asked, "And what do you and Edith get up to after school?"

Josie gave a start, and must have looked guilty, for Miss Rutherford laughed and said, "Don't worry. I'm not checking up on you. But as an ARP Warden I've become very aware of everyone's comings and goings. And Mrs. Prescott says you two often come in quite late, just before Mrs. Felgate gets home."

"Oh, we...meet friends, and play," said Josie. She

felt as if Miss Rutherford had guessed about the bomb-site games – and yet, how could she? She continued, with an air of virtue, "On Wednesdays we go to the Red Cross Cadets group, so we know what to do in an emergency."

Miss Rutherford smiled. "I'm glad to hear that. Do have some more bread and jam. Or will you be in trouble for spoiling your dinner?"

"I probably ought to go," Josie said. "If they're back Aunty Grace will wonder where I am."

"That's true." She got up to see Josie out. "Come again, any time, won't you?"

"Yes. Thank you. And for the tea."

Edith had had a tooth out and was feeling sorry for herself. She had been warned not to run around, so they sat at the top of the stairs and played board games and stroked Biddy and talked. Josie told her cousin about her visit to Miss Rutherford. Edith was jealous of the homemade jam and the look around the attic, but seemed otherwise uninterested in their neighbor, even when Josie described the chaise longue.

Josie did not tell Edith about the Hauptmanns. That was something she needed to think about alone.

Chapter Nine

Tattle-tale

Knowing that Alice was German seemed to explain a number of things. Josie, glancing at the other girl next morning as she wrote steadily and neatly in her exercise book, thought it was no wonder that Alice was strange-looking, that she'd told tales (the Huns had no honor; everyone knew that), that she was so superior and so unfriendly. She probably had divided loyalties.

She wondered if Miss Hallam knew, or Miss Gregory. Miss Gregory was old enough to remember when the shop was Hauptmann's.

Hauptmann. Silently she practiced saying the name. Alice Hauptmann.

Now she knew something about Alice that none of the others knew, not even Edith. That gave her a sense of power. If she told, it would be a gift to them, and it would show that she was someone in her own right – not just Edith's cousin, tagging along. And yet – she also had the power not to tell. And Alice couldn't help being German.

Josie tried not to become involved in the small meannesses, the whispered slurs and covert punches that went on all that morning around Alice. It was a relief to be going to the Red Cross Cadets group after school; she and Edith had to hurry home to get to the church hall on time, so there was no chance to join in anything Pam and the others might be plotting.

As she practiced splinting Edith's imaginary broken

arm, Josie thought again about Ted. He'd be here next week, on Wednesday. Aunty Grace had heard from Mummy and she'd said to Josie, "He can stay overnight – in Peter's room. You'd like that, wouldn't you?" Her face had shown nothing of her disapproval of Ted – but Josie knew.

If only he didn't have to come *here*! She wished she could feel happy about the visit, but instead she was dreading it. She imagined Edith telling the other girls about him: "We've got Josie's brother staying. He's a conscientious objector." Edith had said she wouldn't tell, but she wasn't so friendly now toward Josie at school; she might not be able to resist it. And then the girls would think it was no wonder Josie was spineless. And she'd end up lumped together with Alice.

The next day, Thursday, was the last day of the semester before the Easter break. Josie and Edith set off in good time for school, both cheerful at the thought of the time off. Edith was in particularly high spirits. They were near Ranelagh Gardens when a familiar voice called out, "Hey! Edith! Josie!"

"It's Vic!" Edith smiled and waved.

Vic, with Stan and Ray behind him, had emerged from a side street opposite.

Edith looked around quickly to make sure no family friends or neighbors were watching, then said, "Come on!" and darted across the road. Josie followed.

"Haven't seen you two around for a while," said Vic.

"We got found out – had to see the headmistress." Edith, wide-eyed and indignant, poured out the story. "That girl, Alice – you know, the one we don't like – she sneaked on us. Told the headmistress we'd been on the bomb site. So we're in trouble."

"You want to get her back, then," Vic said.

"We are. We've been getting her every day after school."

"Good for you."

Edith's eyes sparkled. "Except Josie, of course. Josie thinks we shouldn't do it – says it's not fair."

Vic's glance flicked to Josie. "So you're a good girl, are you, Josie?"

Josie felt humiliated by Edith. She liked Vic and wanted him to think she was daring and fun, like her cousin. She said, "It's just that—"

"We think she's a pacifist," said Edith, smiling her dimpled smile and suppressing giggles.

They all laughed. "Pacifist!" mocked Stan. He put his hands together as if in prayer and gazed heavenward.

Josie looked straight at Vic. "Well, I know something about that girl that none of you know."

Now they were all listening to *her*.

"She's a German," Josie said. "Her name isn't really Hampton at all. It's Hauptmann."

"*German!*" Ray's eyes lit up.

But Vic said, "Oh, yeah?" and smirked as if she was making up childish spy stories.

"It's true!" She told them what Miss Rutherford had said, and was rewarded by the gradual change in Vic's expression. Now he looked interested. Edith, she saw, was put out, both at being kept in the dark and at losing Vic's attention.

But the boys' reaction was beginning to frighten Josie. Ray was enthralled. "A German! A family of spies!" And Vic said, "They should be locked up in those camps. They shouldn't be allowed to run a shop."

"It was a long time ago," she said, backtracking now. "They were born here."

"But I bet they support Hitler."

"Yeah – they're still Huns, aren't they?" said Stan.

No one was taking any notice of Edith, and Josie could feel her cousin's annoyance.

"We'll be late for school, Josie," Edith said. "And we've been warned about chatting with boys on the street." She gave Vic another of her smiles.

The two groups separated.

"See you around!" Vic said.

As soon as the boys had gone, Edith turned on Josie. "You never told *me* about Alice being German!"

Josie shrugged. "I only found out on Tuesday. Anyway, you know now."

"Wait till the others hear!" said Edith, already appropriating the story for herself. "We can really get back at Alice now."

"It's not Alice's fault—" Josie began; but Edith withered her with, "Oh, don't be such a *drip*, Josie."

"Heil, Hitler!"

Pam gave Alice the Nazi salute.

The girl looked at her pityingly and turned away. They had cornered her in the toilets at the end of recess.

"Alice! Alice Hauptmann!" said Edith. "Are you a Nazi, Alice?"

"Is your father a spy?" asked Sylvia, giggling nervously as if she half believed it.

Alice tried to push past them. "You're all so stupid," she said.

"No, we're not!" said Clare, barring the doorway.

"You can't fool us anymore. We know who you really are, Alice Hauptmann, and we're going to tell everyone. We know your grandfather's a German. He changed his name, but you can't change who you are. You're still Alice Hauptmann."

"What are you talking about?" But a look of fear crossed Alice's face. She looked, Josie thought, as if she was caught in a trap she didn't understand.

Chapter Ten

"Huns"

That night was cold and clear. There was an air-raid warning, and they all spent three hours in the basement. Edith and Josie took their knitting. Although there was no school the following week, the teachers and the WVS had organized a "Knit for Our Forces" morning on Tuesday. The plan was to encourage the girls to finish their projects and get everything parceled up. A photographer had been promised as an inducement. As they listened to the bombing – which was distant: "Some other poor souls," as Mrs. Prescott put it – Aunty Grace helped Josie with her balaclava and sighed over Edith's scarf. Josie wondered if all the other girls would come on Tuesday. The class was not compulsory. She hoped Alice would stay away; she wasn't sure she could face her.

Good Friday was colder still. In the morning, after a breakfast of porridge and hot cross buns, Aunty Grace took the girls to church. There was frost on the pavement and Josie could see her breath in the air. "It's cold enough for snow," her aunt said.

When they returned to the house there were letters on the mat. Josie watched eagerly as her aunt sorted through them. Daddy, she hoped. Or Ted. She was lucky. Aunty Grace said, "One for you, Josie," and handed her a letter. Ted! At last! She recognized his handwriting. Edith wanted to see, but Josie, still in her coat, ran out to the back garden and climbed the walnut tree to read it in private.

Dear Josie, Ted wrote, *I expect Ma has told you I've got leave next week and will be coming to see you. I'll phone Aunty G. when I know the exact time. Meanwhile here's some news from the depths of Cheshire. I can't believe I've been here two months now* (yes, and not written to me, Josie thought). *Arrived at Chester late evening back in February, needing to get a train to Delamere. Absolute chaos at the station. There had been a direct hit and all services disrupted. People sitting about waiting; WVS handing out tea and sandwiches; fire engines, hosepipes snaking everywhere, broken glass. Nobody knew where to go or what to do. Finally got my train. Shared a carriage with a bunch of Land Army volunteers – girls – and several soldiers. Guess who the girls talked to? They don't even look at a man out of uniform.*

I arrived at my digs late at night, exhausted. As soon as the landlady realized I was a C.O. she said I'd have to go. It's her son, she says. He's due on leave and won't set foot in the house if I'm there. She let me stay the night, but then I spent a miserable day looking for another place.

Several doors slammed on me, but I'm settled here now and it's not too bad.

The work's hard for a desk chap like me! I'd imagined myself felling trees, but we're planting, mostly, putting in tree stakes, erecting fencing, that sort of thing. Only two of us are C.O.s. Most of the men accept us even if they're not exactly friendly. A few are hostile. (Malcolm, the other C.O., got beaten up one evening. But I haven't told Ma that – and don't you.) I like the fresh air and exercise. I'm building up muscles, and the work is useful and I feel good about growing things, taking care of the land.

How's my little sister? I know I made it hard for you back home. I'm sorry about that, but it had to be done. I have hopes that when this war is over we'll all come together and make a better world...

Josie folded the letter and put it in her pocket. It had brought Ted close to her and made her feel homesick. More than ever she longed to see him. But not here. Not now.

Next morning Aunty Grace took the girls shopping. Edith was growing out of all her clothes, and her mother had heard there was to be a sale of fire-damaged cloth at a fabric store in the King's Road.

"We'll go for lunch at The Pheasantry afterwards," she said, "for a treat."

They walked west along the King's Road. The fabric store had big notices outside advertising the sale, and a large number of women had already gathered. Aunty Grace spent a long time looking at fabrics, some with brown burn marks running right through them, some merely dusty and dirty. She held up a dress length in dark blue wool with an orange fleck in it.

"That's horrible!" protested Edith.

Her mother sighed. "You can't be *too* fussy, dear. How about this brown check? It's scorched, but if Mrs. Jenks can cut it carefully…"

Mrs. Jenks had been sewing for the Felgates since the children were babies. Even with a war on, it seemed, she was indispensable.

Aunty Grace continued to rummage. All around, women were buying and chatting. Mostly their talk was about prices, or dressmaking, or the difficulty of managing without their servants, but suddenly Josie heard a buzz of conversation in low, shocked voices from a group of women in a nearby line.

"...broken several windows!"

"And a brick with a message wrapped round it: a swastika and the word 'Huns.'"

"How dreadful!"

"Of course they *were* German," an older woman said. "They changed their name..."

Josie looked at Edith. She had been listening too.

"It's Hampton's," whispered Josie.

"But who – the boys?"

"Yes. That Ray."

"And Vic. Ray's not bright enough on his own."

Josie didn't like to think that Vic would have done such a thing. But it had to be the boys. And she had told them.

"It's my fault," she said. She felt stricken.

"It's nothing to do with you," retorted Edith. "We don't know *who* did it, do we? Could have been anyone." She added, with enthusiasm, "We'll pass Hampton's if we go to The Pheasantry."

They did. Aunty Grace settled on the brown cloth, and as they left she said, "They're saying there's been an attack on Hampton's! Quite upsetting. Such pleasant people..."

The shop was a sad sight. Bombing was one thing, Aunty Grace said, but to see deliberate damage like that – well, it undermined the spirit of the Blitz.

Two windows had been broken and were already boarded up. Inside, furniture had been moved to the back of the shop, but the glass had all been swept up and there was no sign of the brick or the message.

The shop was open. To Josie's alarm, her aunt went in, taking the girls with her, and found the proprietor at the back and spoke to him. Josie was terrified that Alice would appear and accuse them, but there was only Mr. Hampton, her father, who spoke with an English accent and seemed, as Aunty Grace had said, a pleasant man.

"It's one of those things that happen in wartime," he said. "Of course my wife was very upset." He lowered his voice. "We got rid of the message before our children saw it."

Lunch at The Pheasantry was bliss. They had ham sandwiches with radishes and lettuce, and a frosted bun for dessert. All the tables were laid with white damask cloths and silver cutlery, and the waitresses wore white aprons – "almost as if this wretched war wasn't happening," said Aunty Grace.

Josie could not get the sight of Hampton's damaged shopfront out of her mind. Edith was right: none of the girls would have done that; it had to be Vic and his friends. And *she'd* told them; she'd set all this going, just to show off, just to impress Vic and annoy Edith; and now she couldn't stop it. She felt horribly guilty; but mixed up with that was fear that what she had done would somehow get back to Aunty Grace; that Alice would tell her parents what the girls had said to her; or that someone would interrogate Vic and he would name her. And if he did, she realized, Miss Rutherford would become involved too.

She remembered how she had almost told Miss Rutherford about Ted – had felt she might not condemn him, as some people did. And she remembered Miss Rutherford saying, "Come again. Any time."

Did she mean it? I need to talk to someone, Josie thought. Aunty Grace was so restrained and polite; it was difficult to talk to her. But talking to Miss Rutherford wouldn't be easy, either; she'd have to confess what she had done.

On Easter Sunday they went to church again. The church was full of joyful music, flowers, and celebration. Mr. and Mrs. Prescott were there, but not Miss Rutherford. "She never goes," said Aunty Grace, when

Josie asked. Later that day, when her aunt was measuring Edith for the new dress, Josie knew she must seize her opportunity. She slipped out the back way into the garden, and rang Miss Rutherford's bell.

It was a while before she heard footsteps coming down. The door opened. Miss Rutherford looked more homely today, in a pleated skirt and cardigan, and slippers on her feet.

"Josie!" she said.

"I need to talk to you." She must have seemed desperate, for Miss Rutherford said, "Is something wrong?"

"I've *done* something wrong." And Josie felt tears well up and spill down her cheeks.

"You'd better come in and tell me about it," said Miss Rutherford.

Chapter Eleven

Photographs

"I never meant to revive that old story," said Miss Rutherford.

Her back was to Josie as she put the kettle on and reached for some cups. There was a used plate and saucepans beside the sink and vegetable peelings in a colander; evidently she had just finished her dinner. She turned around.

"I shouldn't have told you – only the wrong name

had slipped out. But you should never repeat things that people tell you in confidence."

Her voice was stern.

"I know." Josie began to sniff again.

"Do blow your nose," said Miss Rutherford, making Josie think of the headmistress. She put the cups on a tray, found milk and sugar. "Go and sit on the chaise longue; I know you like that. There's more to this, isn't there? Who *are* these boys? And why did you tell them?"

Josie began to explain: about the bomb site, about Edith and her friends, about Alice, and Vic. ("He's… different, fun. And he *notices* you.") She sniffed again, took off her glasses and cleaned them on her skirt. "It was mean to go after Alice; I know it was. But she's such a drippy sort of girl, and a tattletale, and no one likes her. Edith said it didn't matter."

"Of course it matters," said Miss Rutherford. "But you know that, don't you?"

"Yes."

"Alice is probably just shy."

"She doesn't seem shy. She seems stuck-up – stand-offish."

"Shy people often do. But even if she was a monster: everyone has the right to be treated fairly. Even – well, even Hitler."

Josie looked startled at that.

"We are fighting this war," Miss Rutherford said, "so that decency and goodness prevail. To ensure that no one's rights are taken away; no one is oppressed; no one is bullied or hurt. So even if someone is our enemy we must treat them as we would wish to be treated ourselves."

Josie nodded. "But Edith—"

"Oh! Edith!" Miss Rutherford exclaimed. "Why do you care so much what Edith thinks?"

"I'm scared of what she might say," Josie admitted. She began to explain about Ted, the tribunal, the war work.

As she had hoped, Miss Rutherford did not look shocked.

"I don't have any friends in Greenwich," Josie continued. "My best friend, Kathleen, was evacuated, and everyone else turned against me. I got bullied every day: just words, but horrible words... You can't imagine..."

"Oh, I think I can," said Miss Rutherford. "So when you were sent here it was a fresh start? New people who didn't know?"

"Yes. Only now...Ted's got leave and he's coming to see me. And I want to see him. I really do. But if the others found out – the girls, or Vic..."

Miss Rutherford got up. "Let me show you some photographs."

Josie brightened at once. She liked photographs.

Miss Rutherford opened a cabinet and brought out a leather-bound album. She sat beside Josie on the chaise longue and opened it across both their laps.

Josie was startled to see, not family photographs as she'd expected, but pictures of political demonstrations: large groups of women in old-fashioned long dresses and hats, marching, and holding up placards. "VOTES FOR WOMEN!" the placards demanded. "SUFFRAGE FOR ALL." There were policemen, women chained to railings, women in Trafalgar Square speaking to huge crowds...

"The suffragettes!" she said. "Is that Mrs. Pankhurst?"

"Yes. And that's Sylvia, her daughter; and Christabel... But here, do you see these two young women holding a banner between them?"

"That's you!" exclaimed Josie.

"Yes. And the other one is my friend Violet Cross, who also used to live here. For a year or so, before the last war, we both dedicated our lives to the cause."

Josie began to understand. "Did your friends turn against you?"

"Many of them – yes. And my father was – oh, so upset! And Mother's friends were shocked. It was very distressing. I made my family suffer."

"But you had to."

"Yes. It was the right thing to do. I still believe that. And Ted – you mustn't be ashamed of him. He's doing the right thing too."

"But – you served in the last war. You were a nurse, weren't you? And now you're an air-raid warden. Are *you* a pacifist?"

"I didn't say I agreed with your brother. I said he was right to do what he believed in – not simply to go along with the crowd."

"You're saying I should stick up for Alice Hampton."

"I think *you* are saying that."

Josie looked down at the photographs. The suffragettes didn't go along with the crowd. And yet there, on the march, they *were* a crowd.

It's different for me, she thought. I'm on my own.

But she knew she had to make a stand.

CHAPTER TWELVE

Four Eyes

"What were you doing up there?" demanded Edith. She never liked to feel she was missing out on anything.

"Talking. And looking at photographs."

"Photographs!"

"Miss Rutherford used to be a suffragette."

Edith's eyes widened. "I never knew that! Was she in prison? Did she go on hunger strike? Or chain herself to railings?"

"I don't know."

"You didn't find out much, then."

Josie tried to explain. "I told her about the attack on Hampton's – what I'd said to Vic. We were talking about defending people, and standing up for what you believe in. I told her about Ted as well."

"He'll be here soon, won't he?"

"Wednesday."

Edith smiled. "That'll be fun. Perhaps we'll go out somewhere. And Mummy's sure to do something nice for dinner."

"Ted's not fussy," said Josie. She remembered him, fondly, reading at the dinner table (much to their mother's annoyance), talking politics, hardly aware of what he was eating.

She was conscious that they had strayed from the subject of her talk with Miss Rutherford. She tried again: "Edith, we've got to stop picking on Alice Hampton. It's gone too far."

Edith looked defensive. "*We* didn't throw that brick!

It's nothing to do with us."

"All the same – we should leave her alone now."

Edith shrugged. "She's boring, anyway."

Perhaps the others *will* have grown bored with the game, Josie thought. Perhaps I won't need to stand up for her.

The next day, Monday, the snow finally came: only a brief flurry, but for a while the sky was full and the pavements sparkled under a fine, fast-melting layer.

"In the middle of April!" Aunty Grace exclaimed.

The girls were delighted. They went outside and tried sliding on the pavement, but the snow was too wet. They crossed over to the Embankment and saw both sky and water blotted out, the buildings of Battersea hidden and the barrage balloons like strange monsters emerging from mist.

Josie looked back through the trees at the house and thought how beautiful the scene looked in the softly falling snow. This could be any time, she thought: now, or the future, or a hundred years ago. The house would always be the same.

But by the afternoon the snow had melted.

Tuesday was cold and dull. Edith and Josie put their knitting into bags and set off for school. They did not have to wear uniform today. The knitting session was to take place in the hall, and chairs had been placed randomly. Josie had convinced herself that Alice Hampton would not come, but she was disappointed. As the girls began arriving she saw that Alice was there, and so were Clare, Pam and Sylvia.

Edith went straight to her friends. "Did you hear about Hampton's shop?" They whispered and glanced at Alice, who noticed, and ignored them.

Josie kept away from their talk. She was besieged by guilt.

Miss Hallam called them all to attention, and told them they would spend most of the morning knitting, and then the work would be collected up, stars awarded and photographs taken.

"Anything you haven't finished can wait till after the break," she said. "And since this is not a school day you may sit where you like, and talk if you wish. And we shall also have some singing."

Clare, Pam and Edith began grabbing chairs. They set five of them in a semi-circle, and Josie and Sylvia joined them. Josie saw Alice looking around, uncertain where to sit, unwilling to ask to join a group. She *is* shy, Josie thought; she doesn't know how to make friends. In the end Alice sat on one of the few chairs left, on the fringes of another group, trying to look as if she was part of it.

They all got out their work, and Mrs. Burton from the WVS started them off singing. They sang *Pack up your Troubles*; *Run, Rabbit, Run*; *The White Cliffs of Dover*; and *Jerusalem*. Someone suggested *Whistle While you Work*, and they all sang with loud enthusiasm:

"*Whistle while you work*

Hitler is a twerp

Goering's barmy

So's his army

Whistle while you work..."

When the time was up Josie had finished her balaclava. Edith's scarf came to a natural end and she cast off. Amid much laughter they each put on their own garments (socks went on hands) and Miss Hallam encouraged them to stand close together while a man from the local paper took several photographs. There was a list of names on the wall and everyone who had finished a garment was awarded a star.

At last all the items were put into boxes to be sorted and sent on by the WVS.

The girls began leaving for home. Josie saw Alice going out of the door and willed her to be quickly on her way.

Edith was in a huddle with Pam and Clare.

"We're going to the bomb site," she told Josie a few minutes later.

"The one we went to before?" Josie was alarmed.

"Yes."

"But – we've been warned..."

"The teachers won't know. It's the break. No one can write or complain until we go back, and that's ages."

"I don't think –"

"Oh, come on, Josie. My friends want to go. It'll be something to do."

Josie knew they were hoping the boys would be there. She half hoped that, too; but also half feared it, because of what had happened at Hampton's. But at least, she thought, if we go to the bomb site we won't be pursuing Alice on her way home.

The boys were not there. Some younger children were playing in the ruins, but there was no sign of Vic and his friends. The girls played tag, clambering over the rubble, hiding, shrieking when they were caught. But it was not the same without the boys. If the boys had appeared the shrieks would have been designed to attract their attention; the game would gradually have moved closer to them; and in the end it would have been abandoned in favor of chatting, giggling and showing off. There would have been a sparkle in the air.

But this was just a girls' game that soon became boring. Josie, with her eyes shut, counted to a hundred, opened them, and saw – walking along the road, head down, satchel across her shoulders – Alice Hampton.

She knew what would happen now – and felt a surge of irritation against Alice. Why couldn't the girl have found another way to Belmont Gardens? Perhaps she'd thought her enemies wouldn't dare go to the bomb site again. Well, they'd catch her now.

Pam came out of hiding. "Hey! There's Hauptmann!"

The others emerged.

"She's going to her tutoring."

"Doesn't she know school's closed for Easter?"

"Ve never stop vork. Even on ze vacation."

They began moving toward the girl.

"Oh, leave her alone!"

Josie tried to sound commanding, but she knew it was hopeless. Suddenly the bomb site had ceased to be boring. If they'd had the company of the boys, the girls might not have bothered with Alice; but now Alice would provide the missing excitement.

"Let's get her."

They began to run. Josie shouted, "I'm not coming! Edith, I'm not coming with you!"

But Edith followed her friends.

Josie watched them reach Alice and circle around her. She heard their taunts – "Hauptmann!" "Nazi!" – and saw Alice struggling to push past them. Edith gave a Nazi salute. They sang:

"*Vhistle vhile you vork*

Hauptmann is a tverp…"

Pam seized Alice's bag and tipped its contents on the ground.

It was then that Josie knew she had to do more than stand aside. She ran across the bomb site to where the others had now begun to kick Alice's books around.

"Stop it!" she shouted – with such passion that they were startled and stared at her. "Her family aren't Nazis! You know that. And even if they were" – she began picking up Alice's books and brushing the dirt off them – "it's just stupid! Stupid!"

"Oh, run home to Mummy, Four Eyes!" said Pam. "We don't need you."

Josie had often been called that name before. It always hurt.

"Four Eyes!" echoed Sylvia, giggling.

Josie didn't look at Edith; she was too angry with her. Alice had her books now and was fastening her bookbag as she moved away. Josie walked beside her.

"I'll go with you," she said to Alice. "I won't let them hurt you."

"I'm all right," muttered Alice. She quickened her pace, making Josie run to keep up.

Josie, determined to make amends, scurried beside her.

"I'm all *right*!" Alice snapped. "Leave me alone."

She began to run. And then, suddenly, she stopped and turned around, her eyes wide and pleading. "It wasn't true, was it?" she said. "You made that up about my grandfather? About him changing his name? Didn't you?"

And Josie realized that Alice hadn't known.

CHAPTER THIRTEEN

Brothers and Cousins

She hadn't known, but Josie saw the change in her face as she realized that it must be true.

"I'm sorry," Josie said. "I mean it. I –"

But Alice turned away and ran off.

Josie found herself alone in the street.

She had no friends now, she realized. Her attempt at rescue had not worked out as she'd imagined. Alice hadn't been grateful. And Josie had made enemies of the other girls; even Edith had deserted her.

She walked back to her cousin's house, feeling more hurt and angry at every step.

She rang the bell, keeping her finger on it till Edith opened the door. Edith glowered at her and said, "I'm not deaf."

"No, you're just mean and a bully." Josie went straight to the bedroom, picked up *Jane Eyre* and sat on the bed, pretending to read.

Edith appeared in the doorway. "I suppose you're friends with Alice now?"

"No." Josie held the book in front of her face. "She hates all of us."

"Well, I don't know why you had to make such a scene," retorted Edith. She went out, and Josie heard her calling to the cat: "Biddy! Biddy, come and play! Come on!"

Josie returned to her book, but she could take nothing in. She felt tight and resentful inside.

After a while Edith reappeared with the cat in her arms. "It wasn't *me* that called you names," she said.

"But you went off with them."

"I had to. They're my friends."

Josie began, reluctantly, to understand. Edith was more like her than she'd realized. She too was frightened of becoming an outsider. But surely Edith – so pretty, so confident…?

"You could be friends with anyone," she said.

"But *they're* my friends. They're not usually like this. They're fun."

She put Biddy on the bed next to Josie and both girls began to stroke the cat.

Josie thought about her own guilt. "Alice didn't know the Hamptons had changed their name," she said. She imagined how shocked Alice must have been by the revelation. "You'd think they would have told her."

"Parents never tell you anything," said Edith.

"Mine do." She remembered all the arguments

between her parents and Ted about politics and ideas; and then his decision not to fight. It would have been hard to have kept *that* quiet, but perhaps the Felgates would have. I'm lucky, she realized; luckier than Edith. The thought surprised her.

"Do you think it's her parents that make her go to those extra classes?" Edith asked.

"Probably."

"I'm glad mine aren't like that."

"Me too."

"Well, I still don't like her," Edith said, "so don't expect me to make friends with her."

"I doubt if she'd let you." Josie knew, because she'd been targeted herself, that Alice must have a tight, hurt feeling inside her all the time.

A key sounded in the lock. Aunty Grace was back. They heard her go into the living room and then the kitchen.

"Girls? Are you home?"

Josie got up, and she and Edith went into the

kitchen together. Biddy twined herself around Aunty Grace's legs.

"There you are! How did the knitting go?"

"We both got stars," said Edith. "And our picture will be in the paper next week."

"Oh, splendid! We must order an extra copy for Aunty Winifred." She began unpacking a bag of shopping. "I called in at Melford's on the way home and got some provisions" – she smiled at Josie – "since we have a visitor tomorrow. Everyone was talking about that dreadful business at Hampton's. Apparently the police are looking for three boys; a neighbor saw something and gave a description." She shook her head. "Some of these children just run wild..."

Edith and Josie exchanged guilty glances.

No wonder Vic and the others weren't at the bomb site, Josie thought. They must be lying low.

That afternoon the girls did some cooking in anticipation of Ted's arrival. Aunty Grace had found a recipe for an eggless fruit cake, which involved a much reduced amount of margarine and half a pint of weak tea.

"*Tea?*" said Edith suspiciously.

"It's to make it moist, I expect," said her mother, "instead of the fat. We can try it."

The girls weighed and measured, arguing, giggling and getting in each other's way. Josie's frostiness toward her cousin thawed. Edith can be a beast, she thought; but she's good fun. She stirred the tea and began pouring it into the saucepan.

"Josie!" screeched Edith. "Strain the tea! It says 'well-strained.'"

"Oh!" Josie stopped, tipped the tea back into the pot, and found the strainer.

"Imagine finding tea leaves in your cake!"

"Ugh! All gritty!"

They giggled as Edith stirred.

"Beat it well to get some air into it," advised Aunty Grace.

But when at last it came out of the oven the resulting cake still looked flat and heavy. They left it to cool.

Ted telephoned from Greenwich on Wednesday morning to say he was on his way. Aunty Grace took the call, and Josie, who was in the bedroom, heard her aunt's kind, restrained words of welcome. She longed to rush out and ask to speak to Ted, but she knew it was rude to listen when someone was on the telephone; and of course calls should be kept short – the telephone was not for children to chatter on.

She heard the receiver put down, then her aunt called her. "Ted should be here within the hour," she said. "Now, what are you going to wear?"

Josie thought she *was* wearing something. It had never occurred to her to dress up for Ted. "This?" she asked, glancing down at her skirt.

"Perhaps with a clean sweater," suggested her aunt. "What about your pale blue one?"

Josie agreed. It didn't matter. Whatever she wore, she knew Ted wouldn't notice.

Edith was similarly tidied up, and Aunty Grace bustled about, vacuuming and making beds and plumping up cushions – all the time lamenting the loss of Mrs. White, their daily help, to the armaments factory in Battersea. Biddy fled to the back door and the girls retreated with her into the garden.

It was a beautiful day, warm and sunny. The longed-for spring seemed to have come at last. Josie felt on edge – excited and yet fearful. Would everything be all right? Would Ted fit in, just as he always used to? She was sure Aunty Grace would be polite, but there was an embarrassed note to her voice these days whenever she mentioned Ted. And Josie could not get out of her mind the conversation that Edith had overheard: "Able-bodied young men ought to be doing their bit," Uncle Walter had said.

She and Edith swung and clambered on the walnut tree until Aunty Grace came to the back door and said,

"Now don't get yourselves dirty. Come and help me with the washing. We could hang it outside today."

They climbed down unwillingly. But there *was* something rather satisfying, Josie thought afterward, about seeing the tea towels, dishcloths, vests and petticoats flapping on the line.

Aunty Grace looked up at the cloudless sky. "Such a lovely day!" she said. "It even smells of spring. It gives me hope that this war will soon be over."

The back door was open, and they all heard a loud knock at the front.

"Ted? Already?" Aunty Grace whipped off her apron and hurried indoors, tidying her hair with her hands.

Josie followed, her heart beating fast.

Her aunt opened the front door.

"*Oh!*" she exclaimed.

And Josie saw that the man on the doorstep was not Ted, but her cousin, Peter.

"Peter!" said his mother.

He laughed. "Thought I'd surprise you!"

Peter. Josie tried to swallow her disappointment. Ted would be here soon. But Peter was the one who mattered now: Peter the hero, the Spitfire pilot, the one who was saving his country from invasion, the one who faced death every day.

He swept his mother into a hug, swung a squealing Edith off her feet, then turned to smile at Josie and kiss her cheek. Josie thought how handsome he was in his uniform, with his dark hair and the smile that was so like Edith's. The flat was full of his presence.

"I've got forty-eight hours' leave," he said. "Short notice. I left first thing."

"How long can you stay? Are you tired? Hungry? Josie's staying with us – did I tell you in my last letter? And we're expecting Ted. It'll be quite a party."

Aunty Grace was all of a flutter. And she was on the brink of tears. Josie had never seen her so emotional.

"I can stay till tomorrow afternoon. Don't fuss, Mother."

He followed her into the kitchen as she went to put the kettle on. She was talking about beds. "I was going to put Ted in your room, but we could bring up a camp bed from the basement."

He grinned. "Don't *fuss*. I'm so tired, give me a chair and I'll be asleep in five seconds."

"You must call on the Prescotts while you're here," said his mother. "They'd love to see you. And the Melfords. And the Gorings…"

Peter winked at Josie and Edith. "Would you like to go to the park? Kensington Gardens?"

"Oh, yes!"

"When Ted comes," said Josie.

She'd always liked Peter, but she wished he hadn't arrived first. And she wished it could have been Ted who suggested going to the park.

When the second knock came it *was* Ted. He was dressed in civvies and carried a small duffel and a brown paper bag with a packet of loose tea and some cookies in it – a present for Aunty Grace. He looked a little more tanned than Josie remembered, but otherwise the same as always: a small, slight, earnest young man with fair hair and glasses, a paperback book protruding from his coat pocket.

As Josie hugged him she felt ashamed because she suddenly wanted so much for him to be a serviceman, in uniform, someone she'd feel proud to be seen out with.

The two young men greeted each other, and shook hands. Josie could not fail to notice the constraint between them: each must be wondering how the other would react.

As they drank tea in the living room Peter asked, with polite awkwardness, about Ted's work: where it was, what he did, the details of the planting program. No one asked whether Ted was accepted by the other foresters, whether he had encountered any hostility. The fact of his being a conscientious objector was ignored – rather as one might ignore a disfigurement, Josie thought.

Aunty Grace and Edith asked a lot of questions of Peter about *his* activities, but surprisingly he did not have much to say. Josie had imagined he would have been full of stories of battle and heroics, but he was oddly silent.

Later, when they went out, everything felt more relaxed and normal. They took a bus to Knightsbridge, and walked through Hyde Park to Kensington Gardens.

Josie saw that all the wrought-iron railings had gone. The Albert Memorial was boarded up to protect it, and there were ugly concrete air-raid shelters and gun emplacements. But the paths were still open, and they saw animals: sheep grazing on the grass, and a fenced-off enclosure full of pigs.

The animals all had babies. Josie had only rarely seen lambs before, and she laughed in delight as they sprang around. Edith tried to stroke one, but it ran to its mother, pushing to find her teats. The park was full of the high-pitched bleating of lambs and the lower calls of their mothers.

Ted liked the pigs. "They're comfortable animals," he said; and he leaned on the fence and scratched the head of a big sow, who grunted with pleasure.

Later, they walked by the Serpentine and fed the ducks, and then Aunty Grace sat down and watched as the four younger ones played with a ball on the grass.

After lunch at a restaurant they walked home, and Aunty Grace declared herself exhausted and let the girls make a pot of tea and serve it with slices of their homemade cake.

"Splendid cake!" said Peter. "Interesting flavor. Cinnamon?"

"Tea," said the girls, and giggled.

The last slices soon disappeared.

"You'll spoil your dinner," said Aunty Grace.

But Josie could see that she didn't mind. She'd made a pot pie yesterday and had been concerned about the small amount of meat in it – and that was before Peter arrived.

Afterward Peter was sent to call on the Prescotts, and when he came back Aunty Grace told the girls to leave their brothers to talk and to come and help her. They scrubbed potatoes and carrots and washed and shredded spring greens while Aunty Grace concocted a pudding out of what she could find in the pantry. The radio burbled in the background: "...milk rationed this week, but milk for schools and hospitals will not be affected...oranges and lemons unobtainable...war in Yugoslavia..."

Later, seeing Ted and Peter together, Josie realized that something had happened during that time when they were left talking together. They seemed more at ease with each other now.

At dinnertime Peter went down to the basement and fetched a bottle of wine, and the adults drank a toast to peace on earth.

"And all safe home," said Aunty Grace.

Josie thought of her father, somewhere in France. And Uncle Walter too.

The pot pie stretched to feed five; the pudding – "an experiment," Aunty Grace said modestly – was pronounced a success. They sat chatting afterward, and then Peter said, "We thought we'd go along to the Duke of York, Ted and I. Might meet some of the chaps from school."

And Josie thought: that's brave of Peter; being prepared to be seen with a C.O.

They went out, calling goodbyes to the girls, who would probably be in bed by the time they returned. It was a quarter to nine.

Josie and Edith helped clear the table, and Aunty Grace washed up. Afterward she said, "We should play a game." She was in a happy mood; none of them wanted the festive day to end.

"*Consequences?*" Josie suggested.

"Yes!" Edith ran to fetch paper and pencils – and at that moment the wail of the air-raid siren rose and penetrated every corner of the apartment.

Aunty Grace's relaxed mood vanished instantly.

"Edith!" she called. "Quickly!" She ushered Josie toward the hall, where they met Edith, with Biddy already in her arms.

"Down you go." She opened the door to the basement; and as they hurried down the steps Josie heard the approaching bombers: a sound so loud it seemed to fill the air.

Chapter Fourteen

Chelsea Under Fire

"The boys...Peter..." said Aunty Grace. "I do hope they've reached shelter..."

"It's no distance," said Edith. "They'll be in the pub – in the cellar. Or the Embankment shelters."

"Oh, I wish they were here!" her mother said. "I wish they hadn't gone out."

Miss Rutherford was on duty that night. She called in, noted who was there, and went off to check the other residents and the shelters in the Embankment Gardens. Mr. and Mrs. Prescott came in, and soon they all heard bombs falling and the sound of the anti-aircraft guns starting up.

"Let's hope we get off lightly tonight," said Mr. Prescott.

Aunty Grace no longer felt like playing *Consequences*, so the girls got out the *Blackout!* cards instead. But at a quarter past ten, when the All Clear had still not sounded, Aunty Grace insisted that they go to bed. "You may as well get some sleep while you can," she said.

They went to the two camp beds furthest from the light, undressed to their petticoats and snuggled down under the blankets. For a while they whispered and listened to the murmur of adult voices, the click of knitting needles, and the distant thunder of guns. Once Mr. Prescott went to look outside, and Josie heard him report that the sky was lit up: crackling and sparkling with anti-aircraft shells; crisscrossed with searchlights; flares dropping slowly all around.

The quiet voices resumed, and Josie fell asleep. Later during the night, she became aware of bombing closer at hand. By then it was dark in the room except for a small circle of light from a flashlight: her aunt was reading in bed. Edith was asleep, and the Prescotts had gone back to their own half of the basement.

Josie wondered what the time was. It felt late. She pulled the scratchy blanket over her head and slept again.

She was woken by a massive explosion, so close that it must have been almost next door. It shook the building, and she sat up, her heart pounding.

Everyone was awake now, flashlights switched on, the light revealing startled, frightened faces. Another, even louder, explosion made the room seem to leap and brought plaster showering down on the beds. Josie and Edith both screamed, and Aunty Grace said, "Keep down! Under the blankets!"

Josie could hear timbers creaking. She was terrified

that the house would collapse. The bombardment continued, explosions all around, the anti-aircraft guns going nonstop. The house shook and trembled to its foundations.

Edith got out of bed and went to sit with her arms around her mother, and Aunty Grace signaled to Josie to come to her on the other side. They huddled together with a blanket around the three of them. The most frightening thing, Josie thought, was knowing that Aunty Grace was afraid too; not that she said so, but Josie could feel her trembling.

Mrs. Prescott appeared from the next room, a coat over her nightdress, her face eerily lit by the light from her flashlight. "Are you bearing up? Quite a night, isn't it?" She spoke lightly, but Josie knew she must be frightened.

"The boys – the Duke of York," said Aunty Grace. "I wish we knew what was happening out there."

"Now, don't worry, my dear." Mrs. Prescott came and sat nearby. Her husband joined them. They all wanted to be close together while the bombardment was so intense.

Another explosion shook the room, and Josie clung to her aunt, wondering how much more the house could take. They heard a sliding crash as something fell and shattered outside the basement window.

"Roof tiles," Aunty Grace said. Josie cowered. She expected the ceiling to cave in at any moment. She stuffed her fist in her mouth to try and stop her teeth from chattering. If only Ted was here!

There was no more sleep that night. The battle raged for hours, the guns firing, explosions rocking the building, and all the time the roar of bombers overhead. When the bombardment moved further away the girls were persuaded to go back to bed, but Josie slept fitfully, waking whenever the guns reverberated through the building and the timbers creaked. Every so often Edith would ask, "Mummy? What time is it?" And her mother, who seemed always to be awake, would say, "Two-thirty," "A quarter after three," "Four o'clock," as the hours wore by. In the sealed-up room there was no natural light, but Josie, waking once again, had a sense that it was almost morning when at last they heard the sound of the All Clear.

"Thank God," said her aunt.

They all began to move. Josie dressed hurriedly. It was cold now in the basement and she put on everything, including her coat.

All five of them went up the steps that led to the Felgates' apartment.

There was broken glass in the hall: the small window in the front door had blown in. At the back of the house they saw that the garden was full of debris: wood, a section of fencing, brick rubble. The back door was jammed by some of it.

They returned to the front and opened the door onto a ghostly scene swathed in a rain of brick dust and charred paper. Beyond the Albert Bridge the sun was rising, its light made hazy by the pall of smoke. In the other direction, toward Battersea Bridge, a bomb had exploded in the road a few doors down, blowing in the windows of several houses and leaving a crater surrounded by debris. Gray figures were moving about in the dust. Some of them had formed a human chain to pass buckets of water into houses where the roofs were on fire. Others were sweeping up broken brick and glass, clearing a way through. There was smoldering wreckage in the road from which spurts of flame sprang up; and a choking, acrid smell. They heard a baby crying, the whirr of stirrup pumps, voices calling for more water. A few people wandered helplessly, cut and dazed.

"Girls," said Aunty Grace, "go and put the kettle on. And Edith – find some gauze and bandages: in my emergency box at the bottom of the airing cupboard. Mr. Prescott, I think you should go indoors and rest..."

"Nonsense!" said Mr. Prescott. "There's work to be done. We can start by fetching more pails." And he limped away, followed by his wife.

For the next hour Josie and Edith worked harder than they had ever done before. Aunty Grace brought in shocked and injured neighbors, and Josie brewed endless pots of tea while Edith and Mrs. Prescott washed cuts and grazes and covered them with clean cloth. They comforted small children; found toys for them to play with; offered the use of the telephone, the toilet, emergency food and bedding. Mr. Prescott and Aunty Grace filled pail after pail of water and passed it along the chain until all the fires had been extinguished. The house door stood open and people went in and out across the grand marble-paved hall.

The girls heard of a bomb on the Royal Hospital, another on Cheyne Place auxiliary fire station, which was now out of action. And people spoke of something big – a huge explosion in Old Church Street.

"The Duke of York is near there," Edith said – and Josie thought of Ted and Peter, sheltering in the pub cellar.

But she and Edith stayed at their posts, and so did Aunty Grace, who must have heard the news too.

When all the fires were under control and signs of normality returning, Miss Rutherford appeared in the open front doorway. She was covered in dust from head to foot and swayed on her feet, and she looked, Josie thought, as if she had been struck a great blow.

"Your boys are safe," she told Aunty Grace – and Josie saw her own relief reflected in her aunt's face. "They asked me to tell you. They're helping with the rescue effort."

"What happened up there?" Aunty Grace asked.

"The Old Church. It's gone."

"*Gone?*" Aunty Grace put a hand to her mouth.

"Completely. A landmine. Houses destroyed all around. And five wardens killed in the explosion."

"People you knew?" Aunty Grace took her arm and guided her to a chair.

"Yes. Not my post – but yes, I knew them."

Josie went to fetch more tea, putting in extra sugar

for shock. She had now become tea-maker-in-chief, dispensing to weary aid workers and shocked and injured neighbors. She had two kettles on the go, and three teapots, and the dishwashing was continuous. Edith, meanwhile, although never allowed to use the telephone, turned out to know how, and had made herself useful calling people's workplaces and relatives and passing on messages. Both girls had put their newly learned first-aid skills to good use.

"I hear you two have been indispensable," Miss Rutherford said, when Josie brought her tea and a cookie.

And Josie realized that they had, and had enjoyed it.

"I made a list," Edith told Miss Rutherford, "of the names of all the people who came in. In case anyone asks after them."

"Good work," said Miss Rutherford.

They left her resting, and went with Aunty Grace to look for Peter and Ted.

At the western end of Chelsea Walk they could see

an immense crater. The devastation was so widespread that at first it was difficult to work out what had been there before the bomb struck. Then they realized that it had been the church, several houses on Chelsea Walk and a large part of Old Church Street, which was now completely blocked by rubble. A fragment of brick wall was all that remained of the ancient church.

"It's so sad – so sad," said Aunty Grace.

Josie thought of the church where people had gathered for generations – gone forever. And of those who had died that night.

Some were still trapped. They saw rescue workers bring out the pale, dust-covered body of a woman from one of the damaged houses. It was impossible to tell whether or not she was alive.

A little way off, a gas main was on fire, and small fires were breaking out continually in the smoldering rubble. There were fire engines, cranes and emergency vehicles everywhere; and people, dust-covered and indistinguishable from each other.

But two of the dusty figures were coming toward them, and with a leap of her heart Josie recognized Ted and Peter.

"Ted!" she shouted.

She ran to her brother and he caught her in his arms. Aunty Grace, usually so controlled, astonished Josie by hugging Peter in the street and bursting into tears.

They all began walking back to the house together.

"We've been helping the emergency services," said Peter. "We were first on the scene. When the landmine fell, one wall of the pub blew in, but we managed to get out of the cellar. Someone was trapped in the house next door – two floors had collapsed. Ted managed to reach him – volunteered to lower himself down through a tiny gap between the joists. It could all have caved in at any moment –"

"He makes me sound heroic," said Ted, "but I wasn't. I was just the smallest man there. It had to be me."

"But you did it," said Peter.

They both looked exhausted under their layers of dust. They talked about the events of the night: the rescues; the deaths; the German parachutist who came down on the Embankment and was taken prisoner. "Young – my age," Ted said to Josie. "So ordinary-looking. Someone ran up and kicked him, but that man was led away and the police took the German into custody. But the awful thing is, Josie, *I* wanted to hit him; I felt such anger when I thought of all the death and destruction around us. I could have beaten him senseless. It horrified me to know I could feel like that."

Josie did not know what to say. She took Ted's hand in sympathy.

"You see, we have to get rid of those feelings," Ted said. "We have to see that the Germans are victims too – part of their country's war machine." He smiled. "He's safe now – in a police cell."

Back at the house, the two young men tramped into Aunty Grace's living room, where the carpet was already white with the dust of many shoes. They flung themselves into easy chairs, lay back, and closed their eyes.

"Tea, I think," said Aunty Grace.

And Josie went to put the kettle on again.

Chapter Fifteen

Promises

"Miss Rutherford says I have administrative abilities," said Edith. "She says I'll go far – perhaps run a business."

Edith and Josie were sitting in the walnut tree. Above them the roof was missing a good many tiles, and below, the garden was still full of debris, although the strip of fencing had been removed and the smaller rubbish collected into a pile for burning. The tree rose unharmed above it all. It had no new leaves yet but the tight buds held a promise of spring.

"You impressed her, then," Josie said. She felt rather jealous. Her own tea-making expertise, though much appreciated, was unlikely to have made their new friend feel Josie was destined for great things.

But Edith said, "Oh, so did you! I asked her what she thought you would do, and she said, 'I don't know, Edith. But I do know that Josie will always try to do the *right* thing.'"

"That's not a job," said Josie. But she felt pleased, all the same.

She had introduced Ted to Miss Rutherford; and she knew Miss Rutherford had taken a liking to him. The two of them had talked for a long time about the suffragettes, and the white poppy movement, and the need for change in the world.

Peter and Ted had both slept for most of Thursday morning, then joined the rest of the family and Miss Rutherford for lunch before setting off on their separate journeys in the late afternoon: Ted to Dagenham to see his mother and grandmother; Peter to his base in Norfolk.

Peter came to say goodbye to Josie, and told her, "You'll speak up for your brother, won't you, Josie? He's a brave chap."

She nodded. "Because he rescued that trapped man."

"No, not because of that. That *was* brave, but – well, as he said, it had to be done, and he just happened to be there. But to be a C.O., to stand up for your beliefs when everyone else is rushing into war, to risk ridicule and hatred and put up with it day after day: that's truly brave. I know *I* couldn't do it. You should be proud of him."

I am, thought Josie. And I *will* speak up for him. It would be difficult, she knew; but if Peter and Ted could be brave, so could she.

Edith interrupted her thoughts. "It was fun yesterday, wasn't it? All that first aid and organizing and dishwashing?" She added guiltily, "Of course I know it was dreadful really, but – well, it was exciting and we were all part of it and I felt *useful*. Usually Mummy treats me like a baby because I'm the youngest and Peter and Moira have always been so" – she rolled her eyes – "*wonderfully* clever and well behaved. But they all needed us yesterday, didn't they?"

"Yes. It was good. Better than games."

"Better than collecting shrapnel and going on that stupid bomb site. I shan't go there again." She looked sidelong at Josie. "And I won't let the others call you names again. I promise."

"Thanks." Josie smiled.

"We were horrible to Alice Hampton, weren't we?" Edith said.

"Yes."

"I feel bad about it. Do you think, if we told her we were really, really sorry, that she'd forgive us, and be friends?"

"I don't know." Josie had a feeling it wouldn't be as easy as that. But – "I suppose it wouldn't hurt to try."

Maybe, she thought, if Alice could be drawn out of her shell, she would turn out to be less peculiar and more interesting than they'd thought. She might even be fun.

"Only – I shan't be around," she said. "Not for long, anyway."

Her mother had phoned yesterday, anxious after the night of bombing. She had said Granny was doing well, and Josie might be home in a couple of weeks.

Home. Back to her own neighborhood, to the taunts and name-calling. But I won't mind as much as I did, Josie realized; I'm stronger now. When she thought of all the things that had happened in the last two weeks she felt amazed, and thankful. Perhaps there *would* be time for her to make friends with Alice, after all.

Wartime Abbreviations

During World War II people used a great many abbreviations in everyday speech. On the Home Front, taking care of civilians, were the Air Raid Protection (ARP) wardens and the Women's Voluntary Service (WVS). Women who joined the Forces might be in the Women's Auxiliary Air Force (WAAF) or the Auxiliary Territorial Service (ATS); and bomber pilots such as Peter were in the Royal Air Force (RAF).

A stirrup pump was a device that civilians could keep at home and use to extinguish fires caused by incendiary bombs.

Author's Note

I have always been intrigued by old houses. I've lived in several, and like to imagine (and sometimes find out) who lived there before, and how the house has changed over time.

No. 6, Chelsea Walk, our imaginary house, is based on a real London house, and becomes home to six very different girls. In this story, Josie lives there in 1941, during the Blitz, and I found it fascinating to discover what really happened in Chelsea at that time and to bring some real events to her story, like the bombing of the local church. I hope you enjoy reading it, and recognizing the house and perhaps one or two characters from the other stories in the series.

Ann Turnbull

About the Author

Ann Turnbull knew from an early age that she wanted to be a writer. After working as a secretary for many years, Ann returned to studying and started to train as a teacher. It was then that she rediscovered children's literature and began writing for children herself. Her first novel was published in 1974 and she is now a full-time author. She has written more than thirty books for children and young adults, including *Pigeon Summer* and *No Shame, No Fear*, which have both been shortlisted for prestigious UK children's book awards.

Ann lives with her husband in Shropshire, England.

To find out more about Ann Turnbull, you can visit her website: www.annturnbull.com.

Usborne Quicklinks

For links to websites where you can find out more about life in London during the Blitz in World War Two and other historical events in this book, go to the Usborne Quicklinks website at www.usborne.com/quicklinks and type in the title of this book.

At Usborne Quicklinks you can:

- See bomb damage in London during the Blitz
- Find out more about everyday life from ration cards to air raid drills
- Take a tour of a typical home in 1940s Britain
- Read accounts written by conscientious objectors

Please follow the internet safety guidelines at the Usborne Quicklinks website. Children should be supervised online.

Girls on the Up

LINDA NEWBERY

To Ann and Adèle, with love.
Special thanks to Dorothy Hopkins and to John Liffen of the Science Museum, and of course to Megan Larkin, who started it all off.

Contents

6 Chelsea Walk, 1969

Basement

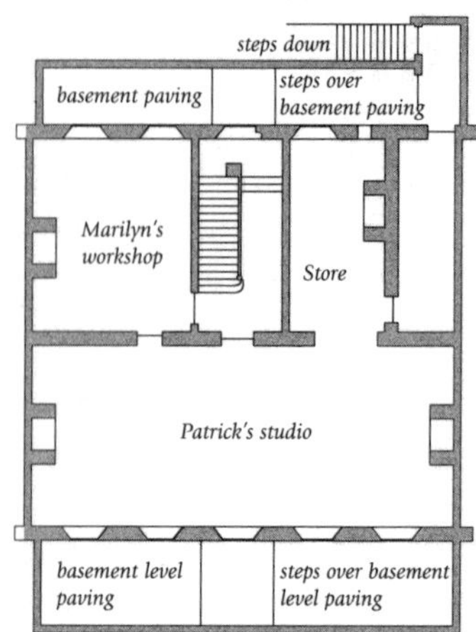

First-floor apartment

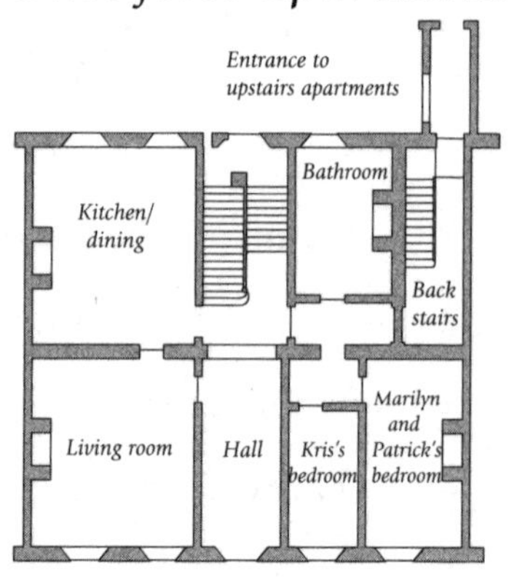

Second-floor apartment

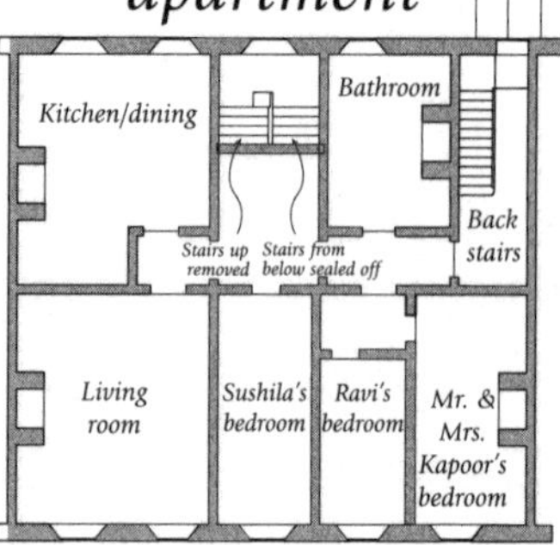

Third-floor apartment

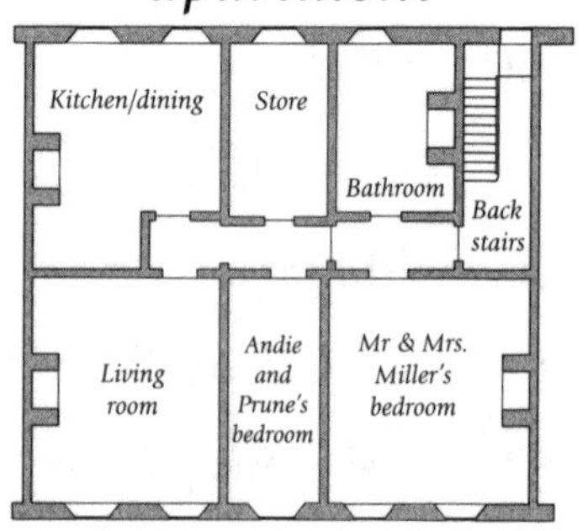

Roof space

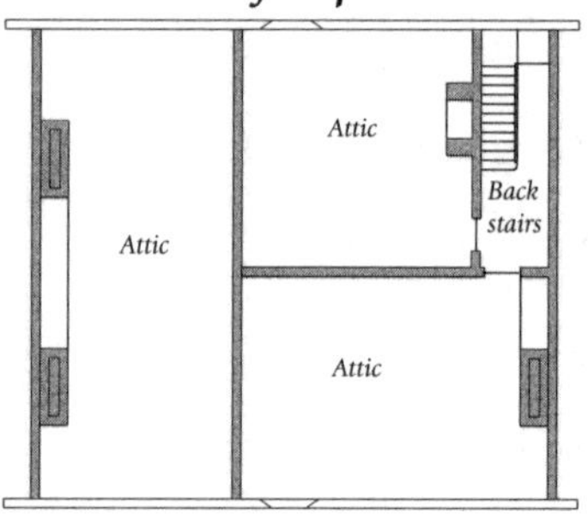

Chapter One

Fly me to the Moon

Andie didn't know where she was – only that something had woken her, and she was staring into darkness.

She sat up, clutching her pillow. The room came into focus: dark shapes of armoire and chest of drawers; tall, light rectangles of curtained windows. It wasn't her own bedroom, cluttered and square, with its one small window where the street light shone in;

this was a much larger space. From the other bed, farthest from the door, came soft steady breathing.

Of course. She was in the Chelsea apartment – this strange new place that seemed so grand and spacious. This was her first night in the room she and Prune were to share, the bedroom that was really Anne Rutherford's. The door to the hall was open, but there were no lights on, so her parents must have gone to bed too. Andie pounded her pillow into a comfortable hollow, rolled over and settled for sleep – then heard, again, the sound that had gotten into her dream and woken her. Across the ceiling, directly above her bed, creaked the slow tread of feet.

She sat up and groped for the switch of her bedside lamp.

"Prune!" she called softly. "*Prune!* There's a burglar or something!"

Prune was a heavy sleeper. Andie had to cross the carpet and shake her by the shoulder before she stirred, and by that time the creaking had stopped.

"Wassamatter?" Prune muttered.

"There's someone creeping about!"

"What? Mmm. *You* are." Prune propped herself on one elbow and pushed her hair out of her eyes.

"No, listen! There's someone on the floor above – I heard footsteps."

"Maybe someone lives up there. Or you were dreaming. Go back to sleep."

Rolling over to face the wall, Prune tugged the sheet up to her ears. Andie climbed back into bed, and looked at her watch. Ten past midnight. Not a sound from above now; maybe she'd only imagined the footsteps. She clicked off the lamp, and lay staring up at the high ceiling, wondering what was beyond it.

That man from downstairs, Patrick, who'd shown them around, had said something about attic rooms where servants used to live, but he hadn't mentioned anyone living there *now.* Why would someone be creeping around the attic at midnight?

Andie felt a shiver of excitement run through her. This was so different from home, which, in comparison to Number Six, Chelsea Walk, seemed very dull – a brick semi-detached, identical to all the others nearby. This house was *old* – built in seventeen hundred and something. Who would even know how many people had lived here, over the years? It had been a big family house, Patrick had told them, before it was divided into apartments. Imagine, one family having this whole huge place to themselves! They must have been incredibly rich. When Andie thought of all the different people who must have walked up and down the stairs and moved through these rooms and slept in the house and breathed its air, she felt dizzy. It was like looking through the wrong end of a telescope, back into history. She was vague about the details, but she imagined a procession of people, their clothes and faces and hair getting more and more old-fashioned, all the way back to seventeen-hundred-and-whatever-it-was. They crowded into her mind, in black-and-white photographs at first, then portraits in oval frames.

Not only did this house have three floors, each one a separate apartment, but it had the attic and a bsement as well – making it, Andie thought, a five-story house, really. As soon as Patrick mentioned the attic, she'd pictured herself sitting up there with her paints and an easel. She didn't *have* an easel, but to be the kind of painter who sat in an attic, she'd need to get one somehow. If it was a bit sparse up there, just bare boards, so much the better. That would make her feel like a real artist.

But the noise. The footsteps.

What if something awful had happened here, and someone was prowling about the attic at night, unhappy, or seeking revenge?

No. Andie didn't believe in ghosts. She definitely didn't.

She pushed back the covers and swung her feet to the carpet. Careful not to wake Prune again, she tiptoed to the window and looked out. She could hear traffic, along the Embankment, and over the nearby bridge; through the foliage of the trees that lined Chelsea Walk she saw the glow of street lamps, and, beyond, the glimmer of water that was the River Thames. At home in Slough, in their cul-de-sac, the nights were quiet apart from the odd late car returning home, but Andie supposed that London never slept. There was a hum of busyness, even at this late hour.

And above it all hung the moon, the full moon, cool and silver, the same moon that Andie saw when she looked up from her own garden at home.

Wasn't there a saying, she thought, about it being unlucky to look at the moon through glass? Or was it only looking at the *new* moon through glass? Not wanting to bring bad luck, not on the first night of her stay in London, she pushed up the lower pane of the sash window and kneeled on the floor, her elbows on the sill. Now she could gaze as much as she wanted, with the night air fresh on her face.

When she was little, Andie pretended to see the Man in the Moon, because Dad used to tell her a story about him. She liked to imagine that the moon's greeny-blue shadows formed the outline of a face, a wise and good-humored face. The Man, she thought, was smiling at her. He was hard to make out, but perhaps that was why not everyone could see him. He only appeared to especially observant people, and Andie liked to think she was one of those.

Now, everyone was talking about man *on* the moon, because in two weeks' time American astronauts would not only fly to the moon, but land there. Just thinking about it gave Andie a thrill of excitement and disbelief. Did the moon *know*?

"Fly me to the Moon" – that was one of the songs on Mum's favorite Frank Sinatra record. The familiar tune started to sing itself in Andie's head; because of Apollo 11, it was always being played on the radio this summer. Soon, flying to the moon wouldn't be the fantasy it had once been. But, gazing at it now –

at *her* moon, the moon she always looked for, and the moon she used to think looked back at her – Andie couldn't quite take in that this was the same place they were aiming for. The moon was Earth's mysterious companion, keeping half of itself always hidden. The space rockets seemed like ropes, lassoes, thrown out to catch and tether it and bring it closer. Apollo 10 had already orbited, with three astronauts aboard, and they'd seen what no human had ever seen before – the far side of the moon.

Mystery, or discovery? Which was better? And could you have *both*?

A moonscape began to form in her mind, sharp, clear and perfect. It was far better than she'd ever be able to achieve with paints and brush; but there it was, demanding to be painted. Tomorrow she'd do it.

She crept back into bed, hearing, as she did so, another small creak from above. Andie froze, listening.

"Prune?" she whispered. "Are you awake?"

But Prune gave no sign of having heard. Andie

stayed where she was for a few more moments, ears straining. Then, hearing no more, she gave up, lay down, and closed her eyes firmly.

Chapter Two

Feet on the Ground

Mungojerrie and Rumpelteazer were the main reason for the Miller family's stay at Chelsea Walk. As Andie was the only one who liked cats, she'd been appointed cat-sitter in chief. She didn't mind that. Forking out Kit-e-Kat twice a day, and keeping the litter tray clean, wasn't much to do in return for staying in a luxurious London apartment.

This kitchen was almost twice as big as the one at

home. Everything was white and gleaming. It looked freshly cleaned when they'd arrived, but the first thing Mum had done was get out rubber gloves and scourers and sponges, to wash and disinfect every surface, faucet and drain.

"You don't have to do that!" Dad told her. "The Rutherfords' cleaner comes every Wednesday."

"You never know." Mum was sprinkling bleach powder in the sink. "It looks very nice, but who knows what germs are lurking? Especially with those cats shedding fleas and hairs everywhere."

The cats, like the apartment, belonged to the Rutherfords, who were partners in the insurance company Dad had now joined. While Mr. and Mrs. Rutherford, with their daughter Anne, were in Manchester to set up a new branch there, and Dad, with his new job in the King's Road office, wanted to move to London, it solved everyone's problems for the Millers to move into Number Six, Chelsea Walk. The house at home was up for sale, and Andie's parents were looking for a house or apartment in Chelsea. Such a move would mean leaving behind friends, school, everything that was familiar – daunting, but exciting.

Meanwhile, neither Andie nor Prune could quite believe their luck at getting an extra two weeks of summer vacation. For Prune, who had just finished her O-Levels, coming to Chelsea was the perfect reward, the closest thing to heaven. According to *Honey* magazine, which Prune devoured every month from cover to cover, Chelsea was the trendy heart of London, the switched-on scene, the hub of the fashion universe. "Maybe I'll get taken on by a modeling agency!" she had told Andie, at least five times. "There are loads of them in Chelsea. What if I turn out to be the next Twiggy or Jean Shrimpton?"

Andie could have pointed out that both Twiggy and Jean Shrimpton were a lot prettier as well as a lot thinner than Prune, so maybe it was as well that she hadn't been asked for her opinion. But she knew that Prune would be doing a lot of hanging around the King's Road – starting today, most likely. Prune hadn't decided yet what to do in September. Dad wanted her to stay on at school (but *which* school? Hillsden High, back in Slough – or, if they moved house, one near here?), while Mum thought she should take a secretarial course. Prune wasn't enthusiastic about either.

Part of the fun of missing school was to think of all the classes you weren't having. Andie ran through her Friday schedule: math, biology, French and English, and finally double art. She felt a little leap of joy inside, at the thought of not being there.

Art was her least favorite lesson. It ought to have been the time of the week she most looked forward to, which made it worse that she hated it. There was something so dispiriting about filing into the big, raftered space on the school's top floor, and hearing Miss Temple's brisk, "Sit down, girls." Art with Miss Temple was deadly. She liked the girls to do still-life drawings or portraits of each other, in pencil or in the powder paints that no matter how thickly you mixed them never kept their brightness on the cheap spongy paper that drained everything of life. The paintbrushes were old and scrubby and looked as if generations of schoolgirls had chewed their wooden ends in frustration. Sometimes, Miss Temple experimented with what she called Modern Art, by which she meant looking at Picasso prints and trying to imitate them by drawing things chopped up into chunks, or viewed from strange angles.

"But Modern Art doesn't mean copying someone else, who's been doing it like that for years and years!" Andie objected. "Modern is *new.* Modern is *now*."

Andie and Miss Temple didn't get along at all. Andie liked to do things her own way, which offended Miss Temple. "When you've spent several years at art college, Andrea, maybe you can come back and tell me how to teach. Until then, I strongly recommend that you do as I tell you." And just being in the same room as Miss Temple sent Andie into one of her dark, depressed moods in which nothing seemed worth doing.

On Andie's report, Miss Temple had written, in her tight, knotty handwriting: *Andrea has considerable talent, but no self-discipline at all.* And a stingy B-, and C- for effort. Andie's friend Barbara, who didn't even *like* art but managed to turn out neat, boring pictures week after week according to Miss Temple's instructions, got B+ and A-.

"Oh, Andie!" Mum said, reading the report. "You really mustn't be obstinate. I don't like you getting into trouble at school."

Andie only took notice of the "considerable talent" bit. Well, that was something, however grudgingly Miss Temple had squeezed out the words. Going to art college was exactly what she had in mind for herself, but Mum and Dad were going to need an awful lot of persuading. "Anything goes, these days. It's all Pop Art now, isn't it?" That was Dad's view. "You can be as good as you like at drawing and painting, but where'll that get you? People do comic-book cartoons, or pictures of soup cans, and call that art."

Mum's line was, "It's a nice hobby, painting. You can do it at evening classes or join a group. But you'll never make money at it."

"Money's not the most important thing there is!" Andie protested.

"No, I know. But you try living without it, and you'll realize that it is *quite* important. When it comes to getting a job, you'll do far better to concentrate on math and English. Then you can learn shorthand and typing. I keep telling Prue, a good grounding like that can get you a job almost anywhere."

"Yes, but only boring jobs in offices!"

"Boring, you may think," retorted Mum, "but office jobs pay well. We wouldn't be going to London, if it wasn't for Dad's job. And as soon as we get there, *I'll* be looking for office work as well. If I decided to sit about all day painting pictures, how would we eat?"

Sometimes Andie gave up arguing; sometimes she

didn't. Mum was like that, always going on about keeping your feet on the ground and not having your head in the clouds. *Gaze at the moon and fall in the gutter*, that was one of her sayings. A silly one, Andie thought. Surely, even if you fell over and grazed your knees or twisted your ankle, it'd be better than plodding along *looking* at the gutter, not raising your eyes any higher to see what was shining in the sky? You'd miss the moon altogether, doing that.

Mum could talk as much as she liked about jobs and offices, but nothing was going to make Andie give up her ambition. How could filing and shorthand-typing ever match the excitement of paint and paper and light?

The Rutherfords' two cats were the haughtiest Andie had ever met. The cat she knew best, Ringo, who belonged to Barbara, would have been purring loudly and twining himself around her legs. Mungojerrie and Rumpelteazer sat upright in their basket and stared in disdain. *You're ten minutes late,* they might as well have said aloud. *We hope you're not planning to make this a habit.*

Mrs. Rutherford had left a long list of instructions, which Andie had already studied carefully but now read again. The cats were to be fed twice a day, at eight in the morning and six in the evening precisely, always from clean dishes. They liked whole milk served at room temperature, and on Sunday evenings they were to have canned sardines as a treat. Both were large and sleek, with velvet collars. Mungojerrie was black with a white chin and whiskers; Rumpelteazer an orange tabby, with a pink nose.

Andie placed the dishes of meat on the cats' special mat, and filled one bowl with water, a second with milk. The rest of today would be free for going out and finding her way around. Later, this evening, the Millers had been invited down to Patrick's apartment to meet everyone who lived in the house.

When the cats had finished picking at their breakfast

of chicken and tuna, and were sitting on the windowsill washing their paws and faces, Andie went to see if Prune was getting up.

She found Prune out of bed, standing by the mirror, turning this way and that. She was wearing a dress Andie hadn't seen before, the color of purple grapes, with a high collar and a very short skirt.

"Hey, is that new?"

"Oh!" Prune turned around, startled. "I thought you were in the bathroom."

"That dress. Is it new? Where did you get it?"

"No, it's, um, not mine." Prune's face flushed red. "I was just trying it on. I found it in a bag on the top shelf of the wardrobe."

"So it belongs to the Rutherford girl!"

"I was only looking." Prune turned away with a flounce. "I haven't got anything to wear tonight, and I found this groovy dress. I'm only trying it on. Isn't it fab? It's from Biba." She posed for the mirror: bare legs splayed, toes turned in, both arms held out to show the fullness of the sleeves, which were gathered into long buttoned cuffs.

"Yes, it looks great," Andie conceded, "but you can't help yourself to other people's clothes! Anyway, what does it matter? We're only going downstairs to meet people."

"But they're *Chelsea* people. I don't want them thinking I'm a complete square."

"So you'd rather they think you're a thief? They've probably seen Anne Rutherford wearing it. And Mum and Dad know it's not yours. They won't let you."

"Oh, don't be boring!" Lovingly, Prune stroked the jersey fabric over her hips.

"I'm just *saying*."

"Oh well, I'll have to get something in the King's Road," said Prune, cheering up. "All those fantastic shops, just round the corner! There's Just Looking, and Bazaar, and Top Gear, and it's not far to the Chelsea Cobbler and Biba and Bus Stop – oh, I can't wait! We can go today!"

"We?" said Andie, suspicious.

"You will come, won't you?" Prune was unbuttoning the cuffs. "I can't go on my own! If Susan was here, she'd come like a shot. But she's not, so I'll have to make do with you."

"Huh," went Andie. "Well, don't think you're doing me a favor. It's the other way round, if you ask me."

She didn't see why Prune couldn't go alone; Andie certainly didn't want Prune trailing behind her when she went to art galleries. Andie *liked* being on her own, but that, she told herself, was because she was an artist and had an artist's temperament.

"When you're my age," said Prune, "you'll be just as keen on fashion as I am."

"No, I won't. What's the *point* of it? Everyone trying to copy everyone else? All those magazines telling you what you can and can't wear? Why can't you decide for yourself?"

"You just don't understand!"

"What's going on in there?" called Mum from the

hallway. "I hope you two aren't arguing already?"

"Nothing!" Hastily, Prune pulled the Biba dress over her head.

In spite of the scorn she exaggerated to annoy Prune, Andie was curious enough about the King's Road to want to see for herself. They had breakfast with Mum, who was dressed in her cream suit, ready to go and sign on with a temp agency.

"I don't know what time I'll be back," she told the girls, "but you've got your key, haven't you, Prue? Don't get lost, and make sure you stay together."

"It's okay, Mum," said Prune. "Andie's twelve, not six. Even if she acts like it sometimes."

"And don't buy anything outrageous," Mum added.

Chapter Three

Moonscape

Andie had been fidgeting by the front window for at least half an hour before Prune emerged from the bedroom, wearing her flower-patterned dress and red sandals, a little crochet bag slung over one shoulder. She had put on makeup; her face was pale, her eyes ringed in black, their lashes thick with mascara.

"About time!" It was a bright, sunshiny day, and Andie was eager to be outside. "I didn't realize you had to do the full works, just to look round a few shops."

"I s'pose you're going just as you are?" Prune glanced disapprovingly at Andie's yellow T-shirt, jeans and sandals.

"What's wrong with it? Anyway, it'll have to do. I'm not changing."

It was less than five minutes' walk to the King's Road, especially at the pace Prune was setting. Prune didn't like walking, but with fashion boutiques ahead of her she was speeding along in top gear.

"Are you sure they'll let us in?" Andie panted, trotting to keep up – her legs were shorter than Prune's.

"Let us in where?"

"To your King's Road. It sounds like a sort of special club, for rich famous beautiful people. They probably don't want dull ordinary people like us. They'll tell us to go somewhere else."

"Don't be daft!" Prune led the way across Flood Street at a brisk trot. "The only thing that makes me look dull and ordinary is having my kid sister with me."

The King's Road, as far as Andie could see, was just an ordinary street with shops on each side, but very busy with traffic and shoppers. There were cafés, some of which had chairs and tables out on the pavement. Prune was trying to look as if she came here all the time, but Andie knew that she was enthralled; it was like walking into the pages of her precious *Honey* magazine. "Oh!" she kept saying. "Look at that! Oh, and see – and let's go in here –" Most of the shops played loud music that thumped out of open doors, so that walking along the pavement felt like passing a succession of parties, each one inviting you in.

Andie couldn't help staring. There was so much to stare *at*. Boys and men with sleek swishy hair and frilled shirts. Girls in thigh-high boots, even on this warm July day. A young man with Afro hair and a tapestry vest, no shirt underneath. Tight velvet slacks, wide-brimmed hats, long strings of wooden beads, short short skirts and a few girls in the new maxi length. *Look at me, look at me,* everyone seemed to be signaling. *I'm young, I'm beautiful, I know what to buy and what to wear, I'm part of this world of fashion and money.* And all the shops clamored for attention: *buy, buy, buy now! Keep up, spend, join the party, get with it!* It was all a bit dizzying.

She knew that, for Prune, it must be a kind of ecstasy that came close to torment: wanting everything at once, not knowing what to choose. "But the prices!" Prune moaned. "I just haven't got enough. D'you think Mum and Dad would give me more pocket money if I asked?"

"Don't be daft! How can they afford it, when Mum hasn't got a job yet?"

Andie thought that even the wax dummies in the shop windows looked disdainful, haughty as the Rutherfords' cats, their hair glossy and straight, their legs long and smooth, with impossibly thin knees and ankles. If that was how you were supposed to look,

Andie thought, looking at her reflection next to Prune's as they gazed in, neither of them matched up very well. She was small for her age, and Prune, though taller, was stocky in build, like Dad, and had wavy brown hair that would never straighten no matter how hard she tried.

Prune gusted out a sigh of pure longing, and ventured into one of the dim, beat-pulsing interiors, to sort through racks of T-shirts and dresses. Andie stayed on the sidewalk. She pulled a small sketchbook and a pencil out of her shoulder bag, and began a quick drawing of the models. She liked their poses, their stalky legs, their blank, mask-like faces, their air of being realer-than-real. Not feeling part of all this, and not knowing how to be, she could at least get something to keep, on paper.

She had finished two sketches and started on a third by the time Prune reappeared. "What are you *doing*?" She sounded irritable. "Why didn't you come in? I wanted to show you some jeans I was trying on."

"Did you buy them?"

"No." Prune was downcast. "Only this belt. There were such groovy clothes in there, And – you should see them! Crushed velvet jeans, tapestry vests, fabulous shoes – but I just can't afford them. How'll I get any decent gear with just my allowance? I've got to get some money from somewhere, or I'll just die! Everyone else is buying stuff – why can't I?"

"Don't be so stupid! Don't *look,* if it makes you such a misery-guts – they're only *clothes,* for goodness' sake!" Andie stuffed her sketchbook and pencil into her bag. "Can we go now? There must be an art shop along here somewhere."

"Hey, that looks interesting – across the street." Prune was caught, instantly mesmerized, by a shop called Scene, whose window was squarely occupied by stern-looking models in red and black clothes. "Let's try there."

By the time they returned to Chelsea Walk, Andie felt as if they'd been in every single shop in the King's

Road, some of them twice. She'd had quite enough of trailing after Prune, having her opinions ignored or ridiculed. At last, even Prune was tired – despondent as well, having bought nothing but the belt, a purple eyeshadow and a new magazine. As they walked home, she treated Andie to a recital of all the things she desperately wanted but couldn't afford. This time it was Andie who was walking faster and faster, Prune trailing, complaining that she had a blister on her heel.

Back indoors, they both gulped down glasses of lemonade. Prune went down to collapse in the garden; Andie got out her acrylic paints and her big sketchbook. With Prune safely out of the way, and the apartment to herself, she began to paint.

The vision she'd had in the middle of the night was still in her mind, clear and strong. She began to sketch the outlines, thinking of the colors she would use. A moonscape, eerie and cold. A dark sky. Floating above, as the astronauts would see it, the Earth, smooth and round as a marble, sea-green, streaked with cloud. Tiredness and grumpiness left her, in the concentration of making pencil and paint do what she wanted.

Chapter Four

Through the Roof

"Oh, Andie, you're not painting in *here*!" Mum fussed. "With that dirty water? What if you spill it, or get paint on the sofa? I'd hate the Rutherfords to think we're not taking care of the place. Couldn't you have done that in the garden? Anyway, it's time to put it all away now, and get ready."

Andie had forgotten that they were going down to Patrick's apartment. She cleaned up quickly – glad for the excuse, really, as the painting just wasn't turning out the way she saw it in her mind – and changed into a clean T-shirt. To reach the ground-floor apartment, they had to go down their own side stairs, outside into Flood Street, around to the very grand front of Chelsea Walk, and in through the gate. A short flight of steps led up to the door. Dad rang the bell, and the others stood behind him on the steps, feeling self-conscious.

"It's ever so elegant," said Mum, tugging at the front of her blouse. "I wonder how anyone can afford to live here? I'm quite sure *we* can't."

"I know." Dad sounded wistful. "I looked at some real estate listings today – the prices are through the roof."

From here, looking down, Andie could see part of the cellar. There were lights on, and music wafted out through the open window.

"But I thought that was the point?" Prune was saying. "That we're going to find a place of our own?"

Before Mum or Dad could answer, the door was

opened by Patrick – the man who'd given them their keys and shown them around when they first arrived. He wore patched, faded jeans and a purple shirt, and his feet were bare.

"Come on in!" He held the door open wide, and they followed him into a spacious hallway with black-and-white checkered marble tiles, and through an archway that led to a wide staircase. "We're all in the kitchen."

Mum was trying not to stare too obviously at everything, but Andie didn't mind gawping. This apartment was very different from the Rutherfords', which was decorated in subdued colors. Here, there were Indian rugs strewn about, and fabric hangings on the wall, beaded and tasseled; the air smelled of incense sticks and spices. Andie was fascinated. In the large kitchen, a woman was stirring something in a saucepan, and fragrant steam filled the air.

"This is Marilyn," said Patrick.

"Marilyn Foley. Hi," said the woman, who was

dressed in a floor-length garment of bright stripes in shades of brown and gold. Her hair was long and mainly loose, some of it pinned up carelessly.

"Pleased to meet you," said Mum, who suddenly looked all wrong in her pleated skirt and slingback shoes. She held out her right arm to shake hands – as if they were at a business meeting! Andie thought – but Marilyn was wiping her hands on a rather stained dish towel, and didn't notice.

"– and you haven't met Kris, have you?" Patrick continued, as a girl in round glasses came into the room. "Kris, this is – er – Dennis and Maureen, that's right, isn't it? – and –"

"Prudence and Andrea," Mum supplied.

"Prue," said Prune.

"Andie," said Andie.

"And I'm Kris with a K. Hi," said Kris, looking at them both with interest. She had a smiley face, and wore jeans and a loose shirt with a vest that could have been made from old curtains.

"Isn't that nice, Andie?" Mum exclaimed. "Someone your own age, living in the same house!"

Andie wanted to shrivel up. Grown-ups ought to know that it hardly ever worked when they said things like that – expecting you to be friends with someone you'd only just met. Besides, it made her feel about eight years old.

"The Kapoors will be down in a minute," Patrick said, fetching glasses. "Amit and Shasha, from the middle flat." He jabbed a finger toward the ceiling. "They've got two children – Ravi, he's twelve, and Sushila, who's about sixteen. Both of them incredibly clever."

"Here, try this punch. I can't remember quite what went into it, but it smells good." Marilyn ladled liquid from the pot into glasses, which Patrick handed around; then she poured sodas for Kris and Andie. The adults began talking about Wimbledon, and today's win for Ann Jones in the women's final.

"Who cares about boring old tennis?" Kris said to

Andie. "I'll show you downstairs, if you want."

"Downstairs?"

"The studio. Where Patrick and Marilyn work."

Studio! That sounded promising. Music studio? Photography? Painting? Following Kris back into the hall, Andie asked, "Do you always call your parents by their first names?"

"Sure, why not?" said Kris. "Patrick's not my father, though. Dad's in America. Patrick's got a son, but he's not around much. It's this way." A wide staircase led up, but Kris went around behind it to a narrow flight that curved down to the cellar.

"Wow!" Andie stopped halfway. It wasn't what she thought of as a cellar, dark and possibly inhabited by rats or mice, but a spacious basement the whole width of the house.

"It's called a half-cellar, really," Kris explained, "because it's only partly below ground level. But that makes it good and light."

The studio was divided into two by open shelving.

Each half, one at the back of the house and one at the front, had its own cabinets and workbenches, and was lit by angled spotlights on the ceiling. Gazing around, Andie saw an easel close to one of the windows, canvases stacked against the wall, ink sketches pinned to a cork board, and shelves of paints, and pens, pencils and brushes in jars.

"That's all Patrick's." Kris waved an arm at the easel. "And this side is Marilyn's. She makes jewelry – she's a silversmith. Have you seen that new arcade in the King's Road? East of the Sun, West of the Moon, it's called. She sells her stuff there. It's cool."

"Yes, Prune and I saw it today. We didn't go in, though."

"Prune? Is that really your sister's name?"

"Prue, she prefers, short for Prudence. Prune's my name for her, but she goes crazy if I say it when anyone can hear. So, Patrick's a painter?" Andie was interested in the easel, which had its back to her. "What does he do?"

"He's a graphic designer," Kris explained. "He does all sorts of things – adverts, sometimes book illustrations or brochures, one or two covers for record albums. He does mixed media, so sometimes he paints, but just as often it's ink or photographs or collage. Right now he's trying to come up with some ideas for a record company. And he teaches a couple of days a week at Chelsea Art College."

"How fantastic!" Andie could hardly believe that she was living in the same house as a real artist. What could be more inspiring?

Kris shrugged. "It's just a job."

"Yes, but –" To Andie, *just a job* was something you did to earn money. Art was more than that. It was a reason for living.

She moved along the workbench, reverently touching the surface, which was marked with paint and scored by knives. Now she could see the paper attached to the easel with bulldog clips. It was divided into squares, and a pencil drawing was beginning to spread from the top right-hand corner, like a plant reaching out tendrils.

"And you?" she asked Kris. "Do you paint or draw or make jewelry?"

"I mess about with it sometimes. Mostly I'm into drama." Kris was already making her way toward the steps. "I do a lot at school, and go to a youth group. How about you? Do you dig Chelsea?"

"Yes! It's so different from where we live, in Slough. The Slough of Despond, Dad calls it sometimes. It's not really that bad."

Kris smiled. "It's the name – Slough! You might as well call a place Swamp or Slump. What hope has it got?"

Andie rather liked *Slough of Despond*, though. With all the moon talk lately, it made her think of something you might find on the lunar surface, like the Sea of Tranquility or the Ocean of Storms. "Anyway," she continued, "there hasn't been much time to explore yet, round here. I want to go to all the art galleries. The museums. And – well, everything."

"Cool. I don't mind going with you, if you want."

"Really?" Andie had convinced herself that she and her family must seem utterly, hopelessly boring to someone like Kris.

"Sure, why not? I've got loads of time now school's finished, and Sophie – she's my best friend – is in France for the whole holidays. We go to Mary Burnet, near Sloane Square. We have to wear straw hats and gingham frocks and knee socks, can you imagine? But it's not bad as schools go, not as prim and proper as you'd think."

Andie giggled, unable to picture Kris in old-fashioned uniform. If Mum and Dad managed to find an affordable apartment or house, then of course she'd have to change schools. It might be fun to go to the same school as Kris, even if she had to dress like someone from Enid Blyton's *Malory Towers* stories.

"You've broken up early," she remarked. "My school doesn't finish till Friday week. I'm missing the last two weeks of term, being here."

"Cool." Kris paused, one hand on the curved

banister. "How about tomorrow? You doing anything?"

"Don't think so."

"Good – we'll go out, then. I can't do Sunday – we're visiting someone. Come on. It sounds like the others are here."

The kitchen was now full of bodies and laughter, bright colors and cooking smells. Marilyn introduced Andie to the new arrivals: Mrs. Kapoor, a handsome woman in an embroidered tunic of ruby silk, and her husband, who wore a formal suit and tie like Dad's. The children, Ravi and Sushila, were both rather beautiful. Their hair was black and shiny, and their eyes were the darkest brown imaginable, under smooth brows. Sushila, who was dressed in Indian clothes like her mother, was already talking to Prune by the Aga; Ravi seemed shy, and had retreated into a corner with a handful of potato chips. When introduced, he said hello to Andie with his eyes fixed on the floor.

Soon Marilyn shooed everyone into the sitting room, which was furnished in rich, dark colors and drapes. She and Patrick brought in food of a kind Andie had never seen before – trays of delicious spicy things, and dips, and little dark-green squarish shapes which Marilyn said were stuffed vine-leaves. Dad heaped his plate; Mum proceeded with caution, nibbling a vine-leaf parcel with great suspicion. Andie tried a bit of everything, liking it all except the olives, which made her think of eyes, and tasted weird.

When everyone had eaten as much as they wanted, there was apple sorbet, served with cinnamon biscuits. Andie and Kris sat together on a big floor-cushion, with Ravi nearby, cross-legged on the floor. Kris took care of the record player, putting on one LP after another. She chose Indian sitar music, and something with a harp, and some jazz – nothing Andie recognized.

After the dishes and plates had been cleared away, Marilyn made coffee and the grown-ups sat chatting. Having dealt with real estate agents and rent, Mum and Dad's list of thrilling conversational subjects had now reached school. "So your two go to St. Dunstan's?" Dad was asking Mrs. Kapoor. "Might that suit Prue and Andrea?"

Patrick passed around a packet of cigarettes, and lit up one for himself and one for Marilyn. Andie's mum, who was supposed to have given up, took one too.

"Come on! Let's go to my halfway place," Kris said to Andie. "The smoke makes my eyes sore."

"What's a halfway place?"

"I'll show you," Kris said, adding, "Coming, Ravi?"

Ravi had been sitting so quietly that Andie had forgotten he was there, but he nodded and stood up.

Kris led the way to the big central flight of stairs. "This staircase used to lead all the way to *your* floor," she told Andie, "before the house was divided up. Now we've got stairs that lead nowhere – see?" She bounded up to a half-landing, then showed Andie how the next three steps faced a blank wall. This landing had been made into a sitting area, with another Indian rug in jewel colors, and cushions scattered about.

"It's my reading place. Reading and thinking. No one bothers me here."

Andie was envious. "You're so lucky! I'm sharing a bedroom with Prune here. At home I've got a room to myself."

"There's always the attic," Kris told her. "Patrick can lend you a key."

"Oh!" Andie remembered the creeping footsteps in the night. "He doesn't work up there, does he?"

"No, he's no need to. He keeps a few boxes of clutter up there, that's all."

"I heard creaky footsteps up there, about midnight. It must have been a ghost," Andie said, half joking, but still wondering.

"No." Ravi was looking at her very seriously. "There's no such thing as ghosts." It was the first time he had spoken to her.

"But," said Andie, "you can't be sure about that, can you?"

"Well, it wasn't Patrick," Kris told them. "He had an

early night, 'cause he'd been out drinking the night before. He was in bed before I was – I heard him snoring. So obviously it *was* a ghost. Our very own ghost. But I've heard it's a friendly one."

She gave a quick, almost furtive glance at Ravi. Andie looked from one to the other; was there something here she wasn't getting? But now Kris was crooning in a spooky voice, holding out both arms with hands dangling. "I am the spirit of Chelsea Walk...*who-oooh!*... I stalk the attic by night..."

"Don't be daft!" Andie giggled, though fear prickled her skin.

"Hey, let's play Murder in the Dark!" said Kris. "We need more people, really, but we can make up special rules for three."

"But it's not properly dark yet," Ravi pointed out.

"I know! We'll pretend it is."

They played Murder until it was Ravi's turn to hide, which he did so successfully that Andie and Kris were still searching for him when the adults came into the hallway, and Andie's dad said it was time to go back to their own apartment.

Darkness *had* fallen by now, and although it wasn't really cold, Andie shivered as she followed her parents in through their side door and up the steep, narrow stairs.

She knew that Kris and Ravi had been hiding something from her, something about the ghost. Maybe it was only a game – or maybe it wasn't.

CHAPTER FIVE

Star-struck

"Here," said Mum, handing Andie two half-crowns. "You'll need to get yourself some sandwiches at lunchtime – I expect they sell them in the museum café. Don't be late back, will you? I imagine Kris knows her way around, but phone us if there's a problem."

They were all getting ready to go out. It was Saturday, and Mum and Dad had decided to visit the Tower of London, something they'd meant to do ever since they were married. Andie and Kris were going to the Science Museum, and Prune was spending the day with Sushila. "She seems a very sensible girl," Mum had remarked. "Lovely manners, both those children."

It suited Andie for Prune to have a new friend. Sushila, being sixteen, was probably as obsessed with fashion as Prune was, so they could hang around the King's Road together. Everyone seemed to have enjoyed Friday night: Andie and Prune because they'd each made a friend, Mum and Dad because the neighbors had been so welcoming. Now the Kapoors had offered to have everyone over in a week or two. "But what about when it's our turn?" Mum fretted; Andie didn't know anyone as determined as Mum to turn everything into a problem. "We'll have to invite them all in *here* – and what will I do about food? I'm no good at those exotic things they gave us. A wine-and-cheese party would be more my sort of thing, or perhaps little egg rolls, and sausages."

"Let's not worry about that till the time comes," said Dad, in weekend mood.

Before leaving the apartment, Andie had to submit to the ritual briefing by Mum: "You won't speak to any strangers, will you? Or go off with anyone? Or stay out too long? Or do anything you know you shouldn't? Promise me, now?"

At last she escaped downstairs to meet Kris. Andie's first choice for their day out would have been the Tate Gallery, but Kris seemed intent on going to the Science Museum: "With all the moon stuff going on, they'll have something special there – and besides, it's near Hyde Park. We can go there after."

Oh well; there would be plenty of other days for going to galleries. Andie fell in with Kris's plans, and they caught a bus to South Kensington.

The Natural History Museum, and the Victoria and Albert across the street, looked like vast, ornate palaces, made of stone. The Science Museum, a more modern building, was in the same street. Kris led the way purposefully inside; Andie gazed around, trying to take in everything at once. Where to start? A plan showed that there were three floors of galleries, with signs pointing to Rail Transport, Electric Power, Children's Gallery.

"Space Technology," Kris said, pointing. "We'll save that till last."

It was fun to have the freedom of the whole museum, with no teacher and no question sheet to fill in. They looked at the giant pendulum in the entrance hall, which was supposed to show how the Earth turned on its axis. "Though," Kris said, "we're not going to stand here long enough to see it happening." They passed quickly through Printing, paused for a while at Time Measurement, then went on to Flying Machines, which ranged from the first spidery contraptions to warplanes and models of modern jet aircraft.

Best of all was the space section. There were replicas of the Russian sputniks that had started the Space

Race, and of the Saturn V rocket that would power the astronauts to the moon. Andie gazed and gazed, and thought how strange it would be when it became real – not just something that was talked and dreamed about. The painting she'd finished early that morning – a moonscape – had turned out well after all, in spite of her struggles the day before, with a kind of accidental eeriness that was better than she'd meant. If Kris hadn't been with her, she'd have made quick drawings in her sketchbook now; but seeing Patrick's studio had made her self-conscious. She didn't want Patrick to know that she thought of herself as an artist. But, then again, why not – mightn't he be able to help her? It would be silly to live in the same house as a real artist and never have the nerve to approach him, wouldn't it? Maybe when she knew Kris better...not yet.

They bought sandwiches and sodas at the café; then Kris said it was time to go. "We can come back another day, if you want. It's free, after all." She seemed to be in a hurry, for some reason.

Out in the sunshine, they crossed Exhibition Road and a wide, traffic-filled street that bordered Hyde Park, with its avenue of trees. Hundreds of people seemed to be making their way in the same direction.

"Is it always this busy?" Andie asked Kris.

Kris laughed. "No. There's something special happening today. Didn't you know? The Rolling Stones are giving a free concert – and there are other bands too. We can't miss it, not when we're so close!"

"You knew all along? Why didn't you *say*?"

Kris grinned. "You might not have been allowed to come."

Well, no. Andie's mum and dad would never have let her; Kris had guessed rightly. But now that they were here, it would be hard to resist joining the drift, just to see what was going on. They were in a green expanse of parkland, with trees and winding paths, so vast that the buildings on the north and east sides looked very far away. Beyond a boating lake, which Kris said was the Serpentine, the grass was clotted with a mass of people. Most sat or sprawled, some with picnics or drinks; others were dancing to the beat of music that came from a distant stage. Andie and Kris made their way through the crowd, trying to find a good vantage-point, but the figures on the stage still looked as tiny as dolls.

"We should have come earlier," said Kris, disappointed. "We're miles away."

"Is that them? The Rolling Stones?"

"No! The other groups will come on first. We can wait, though – we don't have to hurry back, do we?"

Picking their way, they found a place to sit, a very long way from the stage. Every tree had people massed beneath its branches, seeking shade. Andie squinted in the strong sunlight, gazing at the scene in front of her. She liked the Rolling Stones – especially, perhaps, because Mum tutted at them and thought them disgraceful – though she preferred the Beatles, especially George.

Kris offered her a mint. "You heard about Brian

Jones drowning in his swimming pool? He'd already left the Stones, but all the same I wondered if they'd go ahead and play today. It was only three days ago."

Andie nodded. Last week, while they'd been packing at home, she'd found Prune red-eyed and sniffling in her bedroom, listening to the radio. Prune wasn't, as far as Andie knew, a particular fan of the Stones, but for the next twenty-four hours she behaved as if she'd been Brian Jones's most devoted follower. His photograph now filled the space only recently vacated by Paul McCartney on Prune's bedroom wall. Paul McCartney had been taken down in disgrace, having behaved to Prune with unforgivable treachery by marrying Linda Eastman.

At last, to great excitement from the crowd, the Rolling Stones were announced. Tiny figures came onto the stage; Andie strained her eyes to make them out. She had never before seen a real famous person, and now here was Mick Jagger – it must be him – tiny as a distant fairy, and dressed like one, in a white dress with frills, over white trousers.

"Is that really him?" she whispered to Kris. She had the sense that if she blinked, or didn't believe hard enough, he'd disappear, like Tinkerbell.

"You bet!"

Taking the microphone, the figure who was Mick Jagger said something Andie couldn't hear. The audience fell silent while he read from a book.

"A poem for Brian," Kris whispered. "It's so sad."

Mick Jagger opened a box and released a flutter of white that dispersed into the air. It's like that myth about Pandora's box, Andie thought – except that Pandora released badness. What came out of this box was white butterflies. Wouldn't they be bewildered? Where would they go, in all this space? She knew she ought to be sad for Brian Jones, for drowning, but instead she could only think: there's Mick Jagger. I'm looking at him in *real life*. The dazzle of fame made it hard to believe that a starry person like Mick Jagger walked about in the same world as everyone else, breathed the same air, but there he *was*, on the stage.

The mood had changed. The respectful hush that had settled over the crowd was now an expectant pause. Moments later, the volume was turned up and the drums began to pound a heavy, intoxicating rhythm. People began to sway and cheer and wave their arms to the music as the band launched into songs Andie knew: "Jumpin' Jack Flash," "Midnight Rambler," "Street Fighting Man." The last butterflies flickered and vanished like snowflakes in the sun. A passenger plane flew overhead; a naked toddler stamped his feet on the grass and shrieked with laughter; Mick Jagger's voice rose and fell.

A crowd, while it stayed together, was a living thing, with its own mood, its own ways of behaving. Although Andie didn't know anyone here except Kris, it felt like being in an enormous team, or a club – people who had chosen, just for this afternoon, to link themselves through the hum of expectation, the music and the sunshine, the smell of warm grass and the festival atmosphere. Andie had never felt anything like it before. She thought: I'm listening to the Rolling Stones, in Hyde Park with my new friend Kris. She couldn't make it seem quite real.

When it was all over, and the last whoops and applause had faded, people began to get to their feet, looking surprised – realizing where they were, then gathering their belongings ready to walk across the park and wonder about buses or trains back to normal life.

"I don't feel like going home yet," Kris told Andie. "Let's walk over to the lake. We can get ice cream there."

It was the kind of long summer evening that made for lingering. Kris and Andie walked through the dispersing crowd to the Serpentine, and bought raspberry-ripple cones at the stand there. Then Kris wanted to walk home rather than bothering with a bus, and took Andie on a complicated route avoiding all the main roads, instead taking quiet side streets and alleyways. Sometimes she stopped to show Andie an interesting little shop or recording studio, or an art gallery owned by someone Patrick knew.

"Are you allowed to go wherever you want?" Andie asked, rather envious.

Kris shrugged. "Pretty much. I know my way around, and Marilyn trusts me."

It took an age to reach Chelsea Walk. By the time the back of the houses came into view, Andie was tired and thirsty. And she knew that there would be trouble the minute she got in.

Chapter Six

Grounded

Andie and Kris parted at the side gate, and Andie went upstairs, hoping that for some reason her parents had stayed out later than they'd intended. But as soon as she'd turned her key in the lock, she was met by a hail of questions.

"Where've you been? What made you so late?" Mum was hot and flustered. "Why didn't you phone? You must have known we'd be worried!"

"Andie, you really should have rung, if you were going to be as late as this." Dad was less agitated, but still annoyed. "There must have been phones at the Science Museum."

They were all standing in the hallway. Andie pushed past to the kitchen for a glass of water.

"We didn't spend all day there – only this morning. We've been in Hyde Park. I couldn't phone from there. There was this concert – you know, a free concert, with, um, lots of different groups? And Kris wanted to go, and it was free, and—"

"What – you haven't been *there*? It was on the news. You haven't been to see the *Rolling Stones*?" Mum made the words sound despicable. "Andrea, whatever got into you? You know I'd never have let you!"

"What's wrong with it?" Andie felt herself putting on what Mum called her *young madam* voice. "There were hundreds of other people. Anyone could go – we just sat on the grass and listened. It's this big park."

"I know what Hyde Park is, Andrea. But a pop

concert! The Rolling Stones! Who knows what you might have come across? Drug-taking…LSD or whatever they call it…flower people and all kinds of carrying-on I don't even want to think about—"

"Mu-um! Honestly, *you* could have been there, with Dad – you wouldn't have seen anything wrong – and anyway, there were lots of police—"

"Well, that just proves it!" said Mum in triumph. "The police were there for a reason! On the lookout for drug dealers and pickpockets and the like, I don't doubt. And you two young girls on your own, in the middle of all that! Anything could have happened!"

"But it didn't!" Andie humphed. "We just listened like everyone else, and came home. We're not little kids. Kris is *thirteen* –"

"Yes, and I think it was unwise of me to let you go out with her. We hardly know her, and she's obviously got no idea of what's appropriate. You've hardly begun to find your way around, and that's the first place she takes you! And saying you were going to the Science

Museum? I suppose you planned this yesterday, the two of you? You lied to me?"

"Come on now, Maureen!" Dad tried. "There's no need to accuse Andie of telling lies."

"Anyway, I *didn't* lie! We *did* go to the Science Museum, and I didn't *know* Kris wanted to go to Hyde Park!"

Mum didn't look convinced. "All the same, I'm not happy about this. Not happy at all." She rummaged in the cupboard for plates. "Could you go and call Prue, please? She's in the garden, with Sushila. Tell her I've made sandwiches."

Andie went. From experience, she knew that the best thing was to let Mum calm down, then try to pretend nothing had happened. After all, nothing *had.*

The garden behind the house was bigger than the one at home, and was shared by all three apartments. "It's a bit overgrown, especially at the back," Patrick had said last night, "but I like it that way. And it's great for the kids."

"Kids!" Kris had mocked. "*What* kids?"

It was cool out there now, with dusk not far off. Andie had been surprised to find that there were gardens in London, and she liked this private jungly place far more than the begonias and lobelia Dad planted alongside the front path at home. Nothing here was neat. The high brick walls on three sides were clad in honeysuckle and ivy. Straggly roses breathed out their scent; the grass was rough and uncut, and an area at the back was thick with currant and gooseberry bushes, and a herb bed. Nearer the house stood a tall tree – black walnut, Patrick said it was – with a swing hung by ropes from one of its branches. Kiddish or not, Andie would have tried out the swing to see how high she could fly, if it hadn't already been occupied by Sushila. Sushila wasn't swinging, just idly swaying. Her sandals scuffed the bare earth where other feet had worn away the grass. Prune was sprawled on the ground, a cardigan slung around her shoulders.

"Well, *I* would," Prune was saying, as Andie approached.

"I would what?"

Prune looked around, annoyed at Andie for butting in; Sushila smiled and said hello.

"*What* would you do?" Andie repeated.

Prune sighed; she propped herself up, leaning back on both arms. "Since you ask, we were in the King's Road when someone came up to us. Well, up to Sushila. She was from a…a model agency. Andromeda, it's called. She wants Sushila to go and have some photos taken." She gave Andie a tight smile.

"Oh!" Andie swiveled around to look at Sushila. "And will you?"

"Course not. It's probably just a trick," Sushila said. "They'd take the photos and charge me a fortune for them, and that's the last I'd ever hear."

"You could at least *call* them." Prune's voice was thick with envy. "Just to ask."

"But I don't want to be a model," Sushila told her,

swinging gently. "I want to be a doctor."

Prune didn't answer, but plucked a stem of grass and chomped on it.

Andie guessed how it had been: this model agency person homing straight in on Sushila, ignoring poor old Prune. Sushila looked gorgeous enough, just as she was, with messy hair and no makeup, to be on the front cover of *Honey* – you just couldn't help looking at her flawless skin, her dark eyes and the way her smile lit up her face. Isn't that just typical, Andie thought, the way things get dished out? Sushila was not only beautiful, not only brainy enough to want to be a doctor, but – it seemed – nice as well, not at all conceited. Prune was just, well, ordinary. No matter how hard she tried with hair straighteners and foundation and mascara, she'd never look as good as Sushila, even when Sushila did nothing at all. Maybe Prune thought she'd be infected by Sushila's glamor if she hung around with her.

"Did you have a good time, Andie?" Sushila asked.

"Um, yes. Kris and I went to see the Stones in the park."

"Oh! So did we."

Andie looked at her, then at Prune. "*You* went?" She wondered whether Prune would get an earful from Mum, too, when she went in.

"Couldn't miss something like that, could we? Wasn't it fab? Wasn't it just out of this world? And so *sad*, the poem for Brian, the butterflies..." Prune gave a tearful smile.

"Don't start, again," Sushila said, nudging her with one foot. It was like they were already best friends. So Prune had cried in the park – well, Prune would, Andie thought. She could see it now, the kind of crying that's actually quite enjoyable – *look at me, I'm crying.*

Sushila got up from the swing and stretched, then reached for a fringed bag that lay in the grass. "Let's go in now. I'm hungry."

"And Mum's making our tea," Andie remembered to tell Prune.

A small cream card, with *Andromeda* embossed on it in black, lay on the grass where Sushila's bag had been. Andie saw Prune reach out for it. But she didn't give it back to Sushila, or say, "Here, you dropped this." Instead, with a warning look at Andie, she hid it in the palm of her hand, and slid it into her own bag.

Chapter Seven

Ascent

Andie might have guessed. As punishment for going to the Stones concert, she wasn't to be allowed out with Kris for the next few days. "And then," Mum stipulated, after tea, "only if you tell us where you're going, and come back at the time we agree and not a moment later."

"So it's all right for Prune," Andie grumbled, "but I do exactly the same thing and get clobbered for it?"

"Andie, Prue's sixteen," said Mum. "So's Sushila. I can't say I'm delighted about them going, either – but there's a big difference between twelve and sixteen."

"But you're being so *unreasonable*!" Andie clattered the cat dishes into the sink. "What's the point of being in London if I'm not allowed to go anywhere? I might as well go back home and stay with Nan, if I'm going to be kept prisoner here."

"Now *you're* being unreasonable," Mum told her. "Exaggerating ridiculously. No one's locking you in prison. If the agency doesn't come up with work for me tomorrow, I'll take you to Selfridge's. You need new shoes for school."

"Don't want to go to Selfridge's," Andie grumped. "'Specially not to buy stuff for *school*! Not before summer's even started!"

"I know it hasn't. And we're going to enjoy being here," Mum said firmly.

"*Enjoy!* When I'm not allowed out? I bet Marilyn

and Patrick aren't making all this fuss, just for Kris wandering over to Hyde Park!"

"No, I don't suppose they are. But they're – well, much more free and easy than we're used to." Mum made a tight, prim face. "I don't think they're even *married.* He's Patrick Sharp, but her name's Foley, I think she said. All this permissive carry-on we keep hearing about! They're *living together*." She made it sound like a criminal offense. "Not the sort of people we usually mix with."

"You can say that again. They're about five hundred times more interesting."

Mum stood squarely, hands on hips. "Now you're being rude, on top of everything else. I think it's high time you were in bed, young lady. And try to get out on the right side, in the morning."

Andie must have slept for a while – Prune had come in and got ready for bed without disturbing her – but she'd been fully awake for at least half an hour, her mind full of the day's sights and sounds, excitements and arguments.

And now her eyes were wide open, and her ears straining for a sound from the stairs.

She was sure she'd heard something, a creak, like someone trying not to be heard. Yes – there it was, creeping on up, toward the attic.

A tremor ran down Andie's spine – excitement, as much as fear. It could be Patrick, going up to fetch something from one of his boxes, or to put something up there. But why would he do that so late at night, when the whole house was asleep? Only if he had something to hide. What if he was an art thief? Andie's thoughts raced. She imagined Patrick sneaking paintings – small ones, miniatures would be easiest – out of the National Gallery, tucking them inside the front of his jacket. Then he'd store them in the attic until the next dark night, when his accomplice would bring a riverboat to the nearby pier on the Thames, and smuggle them out to sea, to Holland or France…

Or what if it wasn't Patrick at all, but a madwoman who lived in the attic? Patrick's real wife, perhaps – the reason he wasn't married to Marilyn! Andie's class had read *Jane Eyre* this term, and her favorite parts had been about Mr. Rochester's mad wife who roamed the corridors at night and clawed at people with her nails and set fire to bed curtains with the candles she carried. That would be even more exciting than stolen paintings. But if this was the Madwoman of Chelsea, she must be going *back* to the attic, not leaving it...

There was only one way to find out. Before Andie knew she'd decided what to do, her feet swung out of bed onto the rug and nudged themselves into her sandals. A dim light from the street lamp, filtering through curtains, was enough to show her the bedroom door, and out to the hallway. The door to Mum and Dad's bedroom stood open; she heard Dad's snuffles as he turned over.

She mustn't lock herself out! Looking around for something to hold the door ajar, she found a sort of wooden rack with umbrellas in it. She managed to lift it into place without making a loud *thunk*, and slipped past it to the tiny, windowless landing outside.

Compared to the grand staircase that swept up from the ground floor to Kris's halfway place, these stairs were plain and narrow, with a handrail fixed to the wall. After the top-floor landing, where she stood, another flight led to the attic rooms. Looking up, Andie felt the down-draft of dry, dusty air, and shivered. No light was showing. Who – or what – could be creaking around the attic in darkness? And *why*?

For a second she considered going back in, getting back into bed and forgetting she'd heard anything. Perhaps she hadn't. Maybe the sounds were only those of an old house settling into itself, creaking under its own weight, settling for sleep. But then she heard, unmistakably, the sound of footsteps above her head.

Slowly, gripping the handrail, she mounted the stairs. On each one she paused, fumbling for the next with a raised foot. Her eyes and ears were boring into the dark, her heart thumping so strongly that she felt it would throw her off balance. At the turn of the stair she stopped and glanced back at the wedged-open door. If a spectral figure appeared ahead, or if someone flew out at her – a madwoman with nails like daggers – she could scuttle back down and in, and lock the door behind her.

Creak – creak. She couldn't stop the pressure of her feet from making a faint sound, seeming to echo in her ears and up into the roof space.

But what if it were faster than her – the thing up there? It might rush down the stairs and into the apartment ahead of her...shut her out...

Now the creaks were answered by the quick light steps of someone above. Someone moving towards her. She froze, unable after all to run back; fear clamped her feet to the stair, her hand to the rail.

A dark figure appeared in the attic doorway, and stopped there.

"Who's that?" it said, in a quite ordinary voice:

certainly not the way she'd expect a madwoman or a vengeful ghost to sound.

"It's me," Andie told it. "Andie."

The figure seemed to nod. "Shh!" it went, and beckoned her to come on up.

More curious than frightened, Andie followed. A flashlight flicked on, and the dark space sprang into brightness. She was standing, with this other person, on a narrow landing, up in the very top of the house, beneath the slope of the roof. The flashlight beam turned to her face, harsh and dazzling.

"You gave me a fright," said the voice.

Chapter Eight

Skyhopping

"Who's that?" Andie said, blinking.

"Me." The person holding the flashlight swung it back to show his own face. She saw glossy dark hair, brown eyes, white smiling teeth. It was only a boy, and a little shorter than her. Ravi! Ravi Kapoor, from the middle apartment.

"What are you *doing* up here?" She was sagging with relief.

"Skywatching," said Ravi. "Or I will be, in a minute."

"But it's dark!"

"I know! That's the whole point! Wouldn't see much in the daytime, would I?" Ravi shone his flashlight at the bare floorboards, illuminating a telescope and folded tripod, a notepad, and a book called *The Sky at Night*.

Andie was puzzled. There were no windows here, no way out that she could see. "Why from here? Why don't you look out of your own window?"

"Because there's a better view from the roof."

"The roof? You climb the roof in the dark?"

"Haven't you looked up at it, from outside? I don't perch right on top, like an owl. There's this flat bit."

He was picking up his equipment – slinging the tripod over one shoulder by its strap, picking up the telescope with loving care. He nodded toward the book and notepad. "Bring those, if you're coming. You want to come and see, don't you?" he added, a touch impatiently, when she hesitated. He seemed so different from the painfully shy boy he'd been at the party.

"Course," said Andie. It began to seem like an adventure.

Treading softly, Ravi led the way past two open doors that led into rooms stacked with cardboard boxes and crates. "Those used to be maids' bedrooms. No one uses them now. There's this bigger space behind for storing stuff, as well. If it were my house, I'd turn it into an observatory."

Andie was tiptoeing behind. "Are you allowed up here?"

"Well, sort of. I used to come up with Dad. But now I come on my own."

"Is it yours, the telescope?"

"It is now. Here's where we go through." Ravi reached into his pocket for a key, and unlocked a low door in the side of the storeroom. "My uncle gave it to me when he got a better one – he does a lot of birdwatching in India. But this one's quite good. It's a refractor. I got it in January – Dad and I used to come up in the evenings, then. But there's not enough darkness this time of year, so I wake myself up in the night."

Andie followed him through the door, surprised to see a narrow walkway, edged by a low wall. Peering over, she found herself at the front of the house – and saw, a long way down, the garden railings, the gate, and the row of trees that separated Chelsea Walk from the Embankment. It was brighter here than in the attic, because of the street lamps, the lights strung across the Albert Bridge, and the illuminated buildings on the south bank of the Thames.

"Don't look over if it makes you dizzy," said Ravi. "I'm not good with heights."

Andie looked for a few moments longer, to show him that *she* wasn't scared – even though the sight of the long drop made her stomach clench tight.

"It's fantastic!" She turned to face him. "It reminds me of *Mary Poppins* – have you seen it? That song about the rooftops of London?"

"The chimney-sweep's song?" Ravi was moving along the walkway, his flashlight beam shining ahead. "Come on. I usually go round the back. You can't get away from street lights in London, but it's a bit better round the other side."

Andie saw that the walkway led all the way around the top of the house – through a sort of valley between this roof and the one of the next-door house – to the back, where she now looked over the highest branches of the swing tree and over other gardens and roofs and chimneys. There was a steady, low hum of traffic.

Ravi was setting up his tripod, bracing its legs, screwing the telescope to its mount. "There was a bit of cloud earlier, but it's clear now."

Andie had been too busy looking down, and noticing where she was putting her feet, to glance up. Now she did, and the dazzle of stars seemed to fly at her. *Look! Look at us! Why don't you spend every night gazing in wonder? What could be more mysterious, more magnificent than we are?* There were more and more stars as she gazed, as if they were pushing through blackness from as far as her eyes could see. And farther on than that, there would be stars and stars and more stars, and dizzying dark that must go on forever. When Andie's brain tried to stretch far enough to take in the idea of *forever*, it balked and jammed, refusing to believe something so impossible. But that only led to another impossibility: if forever reached an end, what was beyond that?

"Come on," said Ravi. "We'll go skyhopping. It'll be good tonight. Ever done it before?"

Andie stared. "Are you mad?" But what if he really *is?* she thought. What if he thinks we can balance on the wall and stretch out our arms and fly, like Superman to the planet Krypton? Or is he planning to call up some obedient little spacecraft to take us from one twinkling star to another, light years away?

Ravi didn't look mad. He was adjusting the height

of the telescope, swiveling it on its mount, adjusting the eyepiece.

"Skyhopping means getting a fix on a constellation you're sure of, then setting off from there to find others," he explained. "You know the Plough? How to find the Pole Star?"

"I think so," Andie said, not *quite* certain.

"Well, there it is. See?" He pointed. "You don't even need binoculars to find that. See the Big Dipper shape, and Polaris, the very bright one? I've got the scope lined up on that. Have a look. You need to get it right for your own eyesight, so turn this dial till it comes clear."

Andie looked. The stars sprang out at her in fresh brilliance.

"It's part of Ursa Major," Ravi was saying, "the Great Bear. See –" He had opened his book, and now shone the flashlight on a page which showed the constellation in diagram form – though Andie couldn't see much resemblance to a bear. "That's how the first astronomers found their way around the sky. Made their sky-maps. They saw the shapes of birds and swans and bears. And that must be as long ago as there have been people on Earth."

"Where's the moon?" said Andie. "I want to look at the moon."

"We'll have to go round the side."

Andie followed Ravi back into the valley-between-roofs. She was trembling with excitement as he swiveled the telescope and adjusted it. She was about to see the moon as she'd never seen it before.

"There." He stood aside; she moved over to look.

The moon seemed to thrust itself toward her, pale and enormous. She saw its strange, pitted surface so well that she imagined herself standing on it, with powdery moondust at her feet. It had mountains, whole ridges of them, and huge flat plains; it was a *place.*

"Do you think the astronauts will really be able to land there?" she asked Ravi, still peering into the eyepiece.

"Oh, I expect they'll land all right," Ravi said, matter-of-factly. "It's whether they can take off again that I'd be worried about."

Andie looked at him. "Doesn't anyone know?"

"Well, it's never been tried before, has it? They can't be *certain*."

"They must be so brave!" Andie felt a thrill of excitement and fear. "Just imagine, being stranded – looking at the Earth, knowing you can never get back – would you do it, if you had the chance?"

"Like a shot! Wouldn't you?"

Andie thought. "Yes. Yes, I would," she said, after a moment. It felt strange to say this, because in her mind she'd been there already – walked about on the moon's surface, and gazed back at the Earth. But she wasn't going to tell Ravi, because it would sound stupid. In silence, she studied the lunar surface again. She gazed and gazed until she began to shiver, aware for the first time that she was only in her pajamas. Ravi was dressed more warmly in jeans and a sweater.

"I can't believe how close it looks," she said. "As if we could hop over to it and walk about."

"I know. It's nearly a quarter of a million miles away, but that *is* close, compared to anything else we can see. The next nearest thing's Venus, and that's twenty-six million miles, but only at its closest."

"How do you know so much?" she asked him.

"I just read books, and I look at the sky, and notice things and look them up."

"What about sleeping? Don't you sleep?"

"Course – but I'll stay a bit longer. I want to see – hey!"

He broke off as Andie barged into him, startled by a pressure against her legs, a warm furriness.

"The cats!" she exclaimed. "I forgot – I left the door open!"

Panic juddered through her; she felt trembly and stupid. How could she have been so careless?

"What, those big soft kitties?" Ravi flashed his flashlight around, revealing a back view of Rumpelteazer, ginger striped tail held high as he stalked along beside the parapet.

"Rumpelteazer!" Andie whisper-called. "Come here – kitty, kitty! Oh no, I bet they're both out – Mungojerrie! Rumpelteazer!"

"They're not easy names to call out..." Ravi was moving slowly along the walkway on the other side of the door.

Andie's mind was racing. They could go anywhere – escape over the roofs and chimneys of the whole row of Chelsea Walk... She pictured them perched on the highest chimney stack, yowling at the moon like cartoon cats. What if they don't come back? What if they fall? What if –

Slinking after Rumpelteazer, she wondered whether to grab him – but would he skitter away, even scale the roof? Luckily, he seemed less sure of himself out here than he was indoors. He hesitated, looked at her over his shoulder, turned and meowed. She darted forward.

"Gotcha!" She tightened her fingers around his collar, and picked up his heavy, resistant bulk. Carrying him back in triumph, she saw that Ravi had gone inside, to the storeroom. Rumpelteazer's weight made her arms sag as she ducked through the low door. The glow from Ravi's flashlight swept around the room, illuminating beams, cobwebs and more boxes and bundles.

"*Yesss!*" went Ravi, as the light picked out black Mungojerrie stalking a spider in a corner. "Shut the door –"

Andie struggled to do so, her arms full of protesting cat. At least, now, Mungojerrie couldn't go gallivanting over the rooftops. Ravi was stalking him, holding out one hand as if offering a morsel of food. The cat hesitated, his eyes reflecting greenly. Ravi pounced; Mungojerrie yowled and hissed, but he was caught.

Giggling with relief, Andie followed Ravi down the stairs, treading carefully. At the open door of the apartment, she moved the umbrella rack aside and went in; Ravi shoved Mungojerrie through after her. She held the door open just a crack, enough to speak, not wide enough for the cats to slip out again. "Thanks!" she whispered. "I'd better stay in now. But I liked the skyhopping. Can I come next time?"

"Course. I'll tell you when."

"I won't tell anyone if you don't," she added; but he was already ghost-footing up the attic stairs again, heading back to his telescope and the countless millions of stars.

Chapter Nine

Crash-landing

"You know what, And – you're *good*."

Andie looked up from her sketchpad, astonished. It was unusual for Prune to say anything complimentary. But, yes, Andie was pleased with the drawings she'd done of the stilt-legged models in the King's Road shops, with their perfect, haughty faces and their strutty poses.

Prune turned her head to the side for a better look,

adding, "They need better clothes, though. The ones you've given them are just ordinary."

"I don't really do clothes." Andie had just sketched in vague short dresses, or flared slacks.

She was sitting on the garden swing, Prune looking over her shoulder. Evening sunshine filtered through the branches of the walnut tree; pigeons cooed, and a thrush was singing somewhere nearby. It wasn't late, but Andie was tired, after the excitement of the night, and a full day. Mum and Dad, relenting a little, had taken her to the Tate Gallery; they'd spent the whole morning there, then had a sandwich lunch on the Embankment and walked all the way home. Andie's mind was afloat with paintings and sculptures, color and shape – Turner and Blake, Rousseau and Rossetti, and more recent work that was made entirely of dots or wavy lines or bits of metal. Mum and Dad had tutted at those, and moved briskly on to the Turners and Constables, but Andie had wanted to see everything. Now her head was filled with so many images that she hadn't known what to draw first. She had come out to the garden in the hope of seeing either Kris or Ravi, but neither of them seemed to be about. Flicking through her sketchbook, she had found the drawings from Friday, and had just been doodling. But the doodles had turned themselves into a whole series, and her pencil had worked away at them while her mind was elsewhere.

"Could I have some?" Prune asked.

"Have some what?"

"Some of your drawings. You could do them with –" Prune giggled – "with no clothes on. I mean just do the outlines in soft pencil, and I'll add the clothes. I like designing. I've got loads of ideas, but you know how hopeless I am at drawing."

"Well, okay." Andie shrugged, turned a page and started again. If it kept Prune in a good mood, it was worth doing. And it might give her a bargaining tool for later.

Mum's secretarial agency had found her a temp job for the week, shorthand-typing. She was up early to get breakfast for herself and Dad, dressed in her cream suit, and fretting because she said her hair was a mess, although to Andie it looked exactly the same as usual.

"If you go out, you must go together," she told the girls. She was wiping down the drain board, which was already spotless. "Andie, remember what we said about not going out with Kris. And don't be late back. I'll be preparing dinner for half past six and I want you both in long before then."

Andie agreed reluctantly, wondering if she could persuade Prune to catch a bus to the National Gallery. But Prune had other ideas. As soon as Mum and Dad had left, she retreated to the bedroom, where she spent nearly an hour getting ready to go out.

"I'm meeting someone," was all she would say.

"Who?"

"No one you know."

"Can I come?"

"No!"

"Well, that's great! Mum says I can only go out with you, and you don't want me!"

Prune didn't answer, gazing at herself in the mirror, mascara wand in hand. Andie wondered if she'd met a boy; she was certainly going to a lot of trouble with makeup, so it must be someone she wanted to impress. It couldn't be Sushila she was going out with; Sushila and Ravi's school, St. Dunstan's, didn't break up till Friday.

"So what am I supposed to do?" Andie persisted. "Sit indoors all day, on my own? That'll be fun!"

"You can do your painting, can't you? Down in the garden? Then it won't be like staying in. When I get back, we'll go for a walk or something."

"Big deal!" Andie humphed.

When Prune finally left, after examining herself from all angles in the mirror and changing her top three times, Andie went downstairs to see if Kris was in. She was, and suggested doing what she called a "Bridge

Walk": crossing the Thames on the nearest bridge, back on the next, and so on. "We can easily get as far as Westminster Bridge, then we can go in St. James's Park as well. I once did it all the way to the Tower, but it's a bit hot to walk so far."

Andie agreed immediately. She didn't want to tell Kris about the prohibition; it made her feel like a little kid. Anyway, it was quite obviously Prune's fault: *she* was the one not doing what Mum had said. If Andie got in before Mum did, and preferably before Prune as well, no one need know.

It felt seasidey by the river, standing on the Embankment looking down at a passing tourist launch whose wake made ripples that fanned out to the shore. There was even a faint smell of saltwater. Busy traffic crossed the bridge, but along the promenade people were lingering, taking photographs, eating ice cream. Andie liked the mixture of holiday and busy Monday.

"Did you come on your own?" she asked Kris. They were on Westminster Bridge, watching the pleasure launches and the drabber, more workmanlike barges that passed underneath. "That time you walked all the way to the Tower of London?"

"No – that was with Ravi. It was his idea, actually – bridgehopping, he calls it. He's awfully quiet when there are people around, but fun when you get to know him."

What a strange boy he was, Andie thought – bridgehopping, skyhopping! She opened her mouth to tell Kris about her nighttime adventure on the roof, but closed it again and said nothing.

As soon as she let herself into the apartment, she heard Prune crying. Really crying – face down on her bed, sobbing hard.

"Prune! What's wrong?" Andie rushed in, fearing a dreadful accident to Mum or Dad, at the very least.

"Nothing!" Prune turned her face into the pillow, her shoulders heaving.

Andie sat on the bed beside her. "Don't be silly!

What is it? Were you attacked or something? Has something awful happened? Come on, *tell* me!"

Prune continued to sob and gulp for a few moments, then sat up angrily and grabbed at a tissue from the box on her bedside table. "They were horrible, that's what! So horrible!"

"*Who?*"

"The people. The snooty people at the agency."

"Agency? What, Mum's temping agency?"

Prune glared at her. "Don't be dense! You know! The people at Andromeda – the model agency. Sushila wouldn't go, so I went instead – called and made an appointment and they said they'd see me. But they – they –" She started to weep again, tears spilling. Her eyes were already panda-like, smudged with black mascara that made sooty trickles down her cheeks. "They hardly even looked at me! The girl at reception – the way she sneered, you'd think I was something that had crawled in under the door. Then she sent for this other woman, the one who spoke to Sushila in the King's Road. She looks like Marianne Faithfull, only much older – up close you can see her eyes are all wrinkly. She didn't even recognize me! It was only Sushila she was interested in. Just looked me up and down, then said where was my portfolio – photos, she meant. And of course I haven't got any. But then she said – she said –"

"Come on! *What* did she say?"

Prune could hardly get the words out between sobs. "She said – I haven't – haven't – haven't got the looks or the bone structure – or the figure – I'm too *big* – I – I – I could make myself look a lot better but I'm just – just not model material – oh, Andie! You should have seen the way she looked at me, all snooty – like I'm substandard or something, a reject –" She grabbed another tissue and blew her nose hard. "And she went, 'That friend of yours, with those gorgeous exotic looks, we could do something with her. But you're not what we're looking for, I'm afraid, darling.' *Darling!* She really called me darling, only it sounded like an insult. And the reception girl sort of snickered – she didn't think I heard it, but I did – so I just turned round and walked out."

"Well, I'm glad you walked out," Andie said with feeling. "They sound awful! Why'd you want to have anything to do with people like that? As for saying those things – of course you're not substandard! Snobby cow. Don't take any notice."

"But how *can* I not take notice? You don't understand, Andie, you just don't get it – I want to be a model more than anything else, and if I can't do it, I don't know what the point of anything is – and Sushila could do it if she wanted, only she doesn't, and it's such a waste – oh, you don't know how *useless* it makes me feel!"

"Don't be daft! Of course you're not useless. Are you going to let that bossy woman tell you what to think of yourself, just 'cause you're not an identikit Chelsea Girl?"

The answer was obviously *yes* – Prune dissolved

into another tearburst. Andie looked at her in dismay. To be quite honest, Prune looked terrible – her eyes red and puffy, her makeup streaked, her mouth stretched sideways with crying. Andie had been about to say, "That was only one agency. You could try others." But that would surely lead to more disappointments. Prune was never going to turn herself into one of those sleek girls with their racehorse legs and pouty faces and straight glossy hair, the girls she saw every time she opened a magazine or went to the King's Road. Instead, Andie said, "You look nicest when you're just you. When you're not trying to look like everyone else."

"But I *want* to look like everyone else!" Prune wailed.

Andie felt rebuffed. She was doing her best, but nothing she said could make Prune feel any better. She tried to care as much as Prune did, to see how it felt. She thought: it'd be like someone telling me I'll never be any good as an artist, no matter how hard I try.

It'd feel like one of my arms or legs was useless, and might as well be chopped off.

"Come on! You'd better stop crying before Mum and Dad get in," she told Prune. "You don't want them to know where you've been, do you?"

"No," Prune said, in a muffled voice. She got up from the bed, and went through to the bathroom.

Later, in bed, Andie listened for telltale creakings from above, hoping that Ravi might be skyhopping again. Not a sound. Disappointed, she wondered whether to creep out of the apartment and go up to the attic, just in case the door was unlocked and Ravi up there. But while she was still dithering, she fell asleep.

Chapter Ten

Mountains on the Moon

Kris was away for part of the next week, visiting a cousin. With time to herself, Andie painted and painted. She worked at the kitchen table, so that Mum wouldn't fuss about spilled water and stained carpets. Pleased with her moonscape, she made a whole series – fantastical landscapes with rocks and ravines, craters and crevices. She used harsh, bright colors that made the settings look larger than life.

At night, when she looked out of the window at the real moon, it felt like sharing a secret with it. But what sort of secret could it be, when the TV news and the papers were full of the approaching Apollo 11 launch? There were charts, diagrams, interviews, discussions – and it was still more than a week away.

And what about Ravi? When would she have the chance to look at the moon properly again through his telescope, or to stand lost in wonder at the huge spread of blackness and stars? She saw him only once – out in the garden with his mother, who was snipping mint from the herb bed beyond the shrubbery. Ravi had just come from school, and wore a brown blazer and a brown and white striped tie.

"Hello there, Andie! Isn't it a lovely day?" called Mrs. Kapoor, and Andie went over hoping to talk to Ravi. Maybe Mrs. Kapoor would go indoors with the mint; then Andie could ask Ravi when he was next going star-watching. But he only said hello, in an awkward, formal way, then made an excuse and went indoors, and it was Mrs. Kapoor who stayed.

"You'll have to excuse Ravi. He's so shy, especially with girls," she told Andie. "I hope you don't think he's unfriendly. He doesn't mean to be."

But Ravi *hadn't* been unfriendly, or even the slightest bit shy, when they'd been up on the roof! He'd been a different person – confident, fun. Andie was mystified. Had she upset him, somehow? Or only dreamed about being outside with him in the middle of the night?

Prune remained doleful and downcast, though she tried to hide it when Mum or Dad were at home. She lay out in the garden on a towel, trying to get a tan, and complaining that the high walls and the walnut tree gave too much shade; all the same, she managed to get herself sunburned and sore. Without telling Mum, who wouldn't have approved, she had bought herself a bikini – bright pink, with turquoise stripes – but was too self-conscious to let anyone but Andie see her in it. If anyone came into the garden, she made a grab for her towel, and shrouded herself from shoulders to ankles.

Andie did the sketches Prune had asked for, and Prune tried to draw clothes on the models, getting cross and frustrated when the drawings didn't turn out as she wished. "*You* do it, Andie!" She flung down her latest attempts on the kitchen table. "I just can't get them right! I'll tell you what I want, and you can draw it."

Anything for a quiet life, Andie thought. She put her own painting carefully to dry, and drew and drew to Prune's instructions. The results, they both thought, looked good. Andie had expected Prune to want frills and beads and floaty dresses, but the designs were surprisingly tomboyish and practical. Fashions For The Future, Prune called them. Since the clothes could be worn by either boys or girls, Andie developed a face and hairstyle to match – longish sleek hair, and a handsome face that could be either male or female.

On Wednesday, Maria, who was Mrs. Rutherford's cleaner and came once a week, interrupted Andie and Prune in the kitchen. "Hey!" she said, bending to examine the drawings. "Ought to work for a fashion magazine, you two! I could see myself in that jumpsuit, if I lost a pound or two. Very Space Age."

"There, you see," Andie told Prune later. "Even if that stupid agency didn't want you as a model, that's not the only way of working in fashion. You could be a designer."

"Thanks, And. I owe you a favor." Prune collected up the sheets, and put them into a special folder, which she referred to as her portfolio.

Andie was quick to cash in this favor, before Prune forgot or changed her mind. Next day, she asked Prune to go with her to the National Gallery. Prune managed it with barely a complaint, though she got bored fairly soon and sat reading about "How to be a Switched-on Dolly Bird" in her magazine. "Dolly bird!" Andie scoffed. "Haven't you had enough of that? Who wants to be a *doll*? Something to dress up in pretty clothes, and that's all?" But it wasn't worth starting a real argument, not when she was having her own way. They bought sandwiches in the café, then Prune left Andie for an hour and a half while she went to investigate the shops in the nearby Strand. "Nothing like the King's Road," was her verdict. "More like Mum's sort of shops." But Andie had seen Renoir and Pissarro and Monet, and was happy.

That evening Prune went down to see Sushila. Andie was reading in bed when she came back, bringing with her a book called *The New Astronomer.* "Ravi said to give you this. What's going on?"

"Oh, nothing!" With great curiosity, Andie took the book and opened it. "It's…to help with my painting, that's all."

Tucked inside the flyleaf was a small, handwritten note. "*ROOF – TONIGHT – MIDNIGHT*" it said, in sloping capitals.

She could so easily have missed it! Or been asleep, and not even opened the book till tomorrow! Now, tingling with excitement, she prepared to stay awake for the next two-and-a-half hours. She turned the pages, looking at diagrams of the constellations. Maybe, if she concentrated, she could impress Ravi by recognizing some obscure starpattern, or by mentioning that Galileo Galilei, who'd lived near the Leaning Tower of Pisa, had made a telescope good enough to see the mountains of the moon. In 1610! And it was Galileo who thought the moon had seas, though it didn't really, and had named the Sea of Tranquility, where the astronauts would be landing. Of course Ravi would know all that – this was his book – but maybe she could work it casually into the conversation.

Prune got ready for bed, but sat fiddling with her transistor radio; Mum and Dad were still up, watching *Wojeck,* Dad's favorite crime drama. Andie kept an anxious eye on the time. Her parents were usually in bed by eleven, but what if they stayed up late? How would she escape then? At one point, in spite of her worry, she almost dozed off – but then snapped her eyelids open and pushed herself up from the pillow. She dreaded being fast asleep in bed, while Ravi waited for her on the roof. Not that he *would* be waiting, with the night sky for company – Cygnus the Swan, and Sagittarius the archer, and Ursa Major and Minor, which meant Great and Little Bear. It was hard to make herself believe that what looked like scatterings of bright dust was actually made up of distant suns, fixed in their skypatterns. She flicked back to a colored picture of the solar system. The diagram made it look as if some observer had stood right outside the Earth, noting distances and orbits and colors. But, she thought, it's been worked out by people standing just like I did, staring up at the sky – looking and comparing and puzzling – and asking themselves questions about how it could possibly make sense. People used to think the sun went around the Earth, didn't they? – she'd just read that Galileo had even gone to prison, for saying it was the other way around.

How astonishing it was! How had she not been

fascinated ever since she was old enough to gaze up at the sky?

She heard footsteps in the hallway. Mum, in her dressing gown, looked around the door.

"Put your light out now, Andie. It's time you were asleep. Goodnight, love."

It was ten past eleven. Prune was already sleeping. Andie clicked off her bedside lamp and waited until her parents were in their room and the apartment was dark, allowed a little longer for them to fall asleep, then turned her light back on and continued reading.

At last! Five to midnight, and all quiet. While she was putting on socks and sneakers, and pulling a warm sweater over her pajama top, she heard the faint creak that meant Ravi was on his way up to the attic. She tiptoed out of the apartment, remembering to leave the door on the latch this time, so that the cats couldn't escape.

He was there, setting up his tripod on the flat part of the roof. Andie gazed up. The night was beautifully clear, the sky dense with stars – luring her closer, making her wish she could spread her arms and fly into them.

"Hello! It's lovely and clear tonight. I want to look at Lyra," Ravi said, just as if he hadn't virtually ignored her in the garden, last time they'd met. "It's only small but it's got one of the brightest stars in it, Vega."

"Does Kris know you come out here?" Andie asked, while he was adjusting the telescope.

"Course! That's why she was winding you up about the ghost. She knew it was me," Ravi said, with his shy grin.

"Wouldn't she want to come, too? I mean, Patrick and Marilyn let her do whatever she wants – she wouldn't have to sneak out, like I do."

"She did come up a couple of times. But she's no good at staying awake, or waking up once she's gone to sleep – and when she did, she had to stay in bed till ten in the morning, to get over it."

"It's just – you know," Andie tried, "I don't want to leave her out."

Ravi looked at her in surprise. "Leave her out? Who's leaving her out? She's not interested, and we are, that's all. But I was telling you about Vega. You can't miss it, even with just your eyes – it's the fifth brightest star of all. Fifty times brighter than our sun. That's a useful one for skyhopping. Here, look through the scope. See it, the really bright one?"

"Yes, I think so."

"And if you look really closely at Delta," Ravi continued, "which is left and a little bit down, you'll see that it's really a double! Can you see the two separate stars, very close together?"

"Yes!" Andie said, after searching for a few moments. "And they're different colors – one's sort of reddish, and the other one's white."

"That's right. Now look with just your eyes, and I'll show you the Summer Triangle – a triangle made by Vega and two other bright stars, Deneb and Altair.

That's useful to know, as well...gives you a good, er, landmark..."

"Skymark?"

"Okay then, skymark."

Soon Andie had various skymarks she could pick out for herself – even if she'd never know as many stars by name as Ravi did.

"But they're moving!" she exclaimed, finding that she had to keep making slight turns of the telescope.

"They're not. *We* are. The Earth's turning – the stars stay where they are."

"Well, course." Andie tried to pretend she'd always known this. And of course she *had* known – but how odd to see it happening, almost to feel it!

"Now let's come a lot closer to home," Ravi said, when Andie was quite dazzled. "To the moon, I mean."

He positioned the tripod and focused, muttering, sounding pleased, then motioned Andie toward the eyepiece. As before, the moon's surface leaped toward her, startling in its detail. It wasn't just a decoration in the sky, a flat silver disk like a floating coin, or smooth like a Christmas-tree decoration. It was real, huge, *there* – the telescope brought its surface features sharply into view, mountain ridges, craters, peaks, valleys, cracks. Some parts looked as dimpled as orange peel, some were craggy with cliffs or smooth as lakes. Andie had just seen in the book that all the mountains and craters and plains had names; there were detailed maps. Some astronomers, it seemed, knew the moon better than Andie knew the back garden at home.

"I feel dizzy." She stepped back from the telescope at last. "Moon-dazzled."

"That's the best kind of dazzled," Ravi said, taking over. "Next to sky-dazed, or star-giddy."

Andie looked up. It was true – the stars did make her giddy, as her eyes reached farther into their depths, and more and more of them seemed to rain at her, pouring through the immensity. She stretched out her hands and saw stars shining between her spread fingers:

worlds and worlds contained in the span of a hand. I'm starbathing, she thought. Better than sunbathing – that only makes you hot and red. Starbathing fills you with time and space and wonder.

She tried to do it in paint – to show the blackness of space, pricked by points of light as far as the eye could see, and the mystery of *forever*. But paint just wouldn't do it. It was only a spotty mess. Every time she thought she was getting better at painting – every time she did something she felt proud of – her next attempt would show her how much she just couldn't do. Her eyes saw, and her mind saw, but in between them and the paper were her clumsy hands.

Sometimes she felt like giving up. But only sometimes.

Chapter Eleven

East of the Sun, West of the Moon

Prune's birthday was coming soon. As Prune had such definite ideas about what she liked and didn't like, Andie thought it would be safest to let her choose her own present. This meant a shopping trip, to look for something Andie could afford – a record, perhaps, or a rope of beads or some bangles. Andie braced herself for a morning of watching Prune drool over things she couldn't have, and off they went to the King's Road.

The present was found and bought with surprising ease – a Simon and Garfunkel album, which cost more than Andie had had in mind, but was very definitely what Prune wanted. But, of course, Prune hadn't finished yet.

"I want to look in East of the Sun, West of the Moon." She grabbed Andie's arm; not waiting for an answer, she pulled and shoved her through stationary traffic to the shop entrance on the other side of the road.

A lanky young man, with straggly hair and a beard that made Andie think of paintings of Jesus, stood by the open frontage, smoking and gazing out into the street. His thoughts seemed to be elsewhere; he gave the girls a vague nod as they passed. Prune marched straight in; Andie followed, feeling like someone entering a different, intriguing world, like Narnia. East of the Sun, West of the Moon wasn't just one shop, but a sort of indoor market, made up of separate stalls, some with their own entrance doors or bead curtains.

Inside was shadowy and enticing, smelling headily of incense sticks and patchouli and cotton, lit with tiny lamps strung around the ceiling and from the partitions. Andie saw rugs in earthy colors, kaftans, belts and beads, mirrored cushions, colorful bowls; sitar music lured her farther in. A few customers were browsing, but no sales staff were in evidence.

"Marilyn's jewelry's in here," Andie reminded Prune. "You know, Kris's mum."

Jewelry of various kinds was mounted on a stand at the very back of the arcade. Andie and Prune gazed at rings, necklaces, beads, bangles, chokers and earrings, displayed against a backdrop of midnight-blue velvet. Marilyn's pieces, pinned to a board headed *Foleyworks*, were of finely-wrought silver in the shapes of fish, snakes, moons and twining patterns, some studded with tiny gemstones of turquoise or black. Also on the stand were heavier pieces by other designers – made from bronze, gold or wood, decorated with shells, feathers and many-colored beads.

"Oh! I love this – I just love it!" Prune lifted a carved ivory bracelet and slipped her hand through it, turning her wrist this way and that. "I saw one just like this in *Honey*, with a safari jacket and skirt. Doesn't it look great?"

"How much?"

Prune flipped over the small handwritten price-tag. "Fifteen pounds! But it *is* real ivory."

"No one in their right mind would spend that much on a *bracelet*," Andie said. "Anyway, it's dead elephant. You wouldn't wear dead elephant, would you?"

"No-o." Prune sounded doubtful, but took off the bracelet and replaced it on the stand.

They wandered on, Prune to a rack of tie-dye T-shirts, Andie to a stall draped with silky Indian scarves. Prune took ages, dismissing half the clothes, examining others with minute detail, then finally choosing a tiger's-eye ring from the jewelry stall.

"Come on!" Andie was impatient. "I'm hungry.

Let's go home and get some lunch." She looked around for someone to take Prune's money. There seemed to be only the Jesus-man, who was still standing by the door smoking as if he had nothing else to do. She wasn't even sure that he worked here; but as they approached, he moved to a cash register on the nearby counter.

"Just this, please." Prune took a ten-shilling note out of her purse to pay for the ring.

The man gave her half-a-crown change, then looked at her searchingly and said, "Just by the way, what about the bangle?"

Prune's cheeks flushed red. "What bangle?"

"The one in your bag. Are you thinking of paying for that as well?"

"I don't know what you mean," Prune stammered.

Andie looked at her, aghast. She knew Prune well enough to recognize guilt when she saw it. The young man really did look quite a lot like Jesus, or at least how Andie imagined Jesus to look. He had sad hazel eyes that rested reproachfully on Prune's face, and thin cheeks as if he didn't get enough to eat. He was even wearing a thin and slightly dirty white kaftan that looked a bit Biblical.

"Hey," he said. "I saw you slip that bangle into your bag when you thought no one was looking. I'm not going to get heavy about it. It's no big deal to me. It's only money when it comes down to it, and there's more important things to worry about. It's your conscience, not mine. Who's to say a thing belongs to one person rather than another, just 'cause he's paid money for it? If you want it that badly, take it – go on. I'm just telling you that I *know*."

Andie was fascinated. Prune, turning ever-brighter scarlet, looked incapable of saying anything at all, so Andie put in, "Actually, if that bangle belongs to anyone, it's the elephant whose tusks it's made out of. I don't see why people should cut off bits of animal to make jewelry, when there are other things they could just as easily use."

The Jesus-man looked at her with interest. "Well, you've got a point there. I can dig that. See, I don't eat animals, or wear animals, or use anything from animals. But hey, who said it was an ivory bangle? I didn't."

"Well, I –" Now it was Andie's turn to feel her face firing up. He must think *she* was involved in this. "Why are you selling ivory, then, if you don't want to use animal stuff? That doesn't make much sense!"

"It's not my shop," he said pleasantly. "I'm just standing in for a friend who's gone traveling."

Andie couldn't quite see where the conversation had gotten to, or how it might end. This young man wasn't actually asking Prune to turn out her bag, or threatening to call the police. And Prune wasn't marching out of the shop in a temper, or trying to make a run for it – but she wasn't denying having the bangle, either, which would surely be her response if she *hadn't* got it.

"Come on, Prune!" Andie said, impatient to be gone.

"Have you got it, or haven't you?"

"Prune, was that?" The Jesus-man was leaning on the counter with both elbows. He had a very nice smile, Andie noticed.

"Prudence. Prue. Anything but Prune," Prune said, flustered. She reached into her crochet bag, and, shamefaced, drew out the carved bangle and handed it over. "I'm sorry – I must have—"

"Zak? What's going on?" called a female voice. There was a jangle of bead curtains behind the register, and a wild-haired woman with an Indian scarf tied as a headband came through to join the Jesus-man. Unlike him, she had a very businesslike manner, and piercing blue eyes that seemed to take in the situation at one glance.

"Oh, nothing. We were just chatting," he said. He covered the bangle with his hand, and pushed it under a folded scarf near the register.

Andie gave him a *thank you* look, said goodbye and hurried Prune out to the sidewalk.

"What's got *into* you?" she hissed. A girl burdened with grocery bags tutted as she veered around them into the road. "Prune? Were you really going to *steal* that?"

"I don't know! I – I – no, of course not! I must have put it in my bag by mistake."

"Really?" Andie peered at her closely. "Well, you were lucky that Zak guy was so un-heavy about it. You could have been arrested! Prune, you can't go round helping yourself to stuff!"

"I don't!"

"Not much, you don't. It's like that Biba dress in the wardrobe. You see something and you've just got to have it. Honestly, you shouldn't be allowed out!"

"It was a mistake!" Prune flared back. "Don't you ever make a mistake?"

"Not mistakes that make me steal from shops, no!"

They'd started to walk in the direction of the Town Hall, but now Prune stopped, taking hold of Andie's sleeve. "Andie – you won't tell Mum, will you? Or Dad?"

"No," said Andie, "as long as you promise not to do it again. By mistake or on purpose. I don't want a jailbird for a sister, thanks."

"He was nice, though, that Zak, wasn't he? Weird, but nice."

"Yeah," Andie retorted, "and I bet he thought you were really great. Trying to nick stuff, then standing there red as a beet. A gibbering beet."

"I didn't gibber!"

"Yes, you did. It's a good job I was there, or you'd have melted into a bright red gibbering jelly."

Very huffy with each other, they walked home in silence.

CHAPTER TWELVE

Everyone's Gone to the Moon

By Sunday, the ban on going out with Kris had expired. Kris came up to see if Andie wanted to go to Hyde Park again – not for a rock concert this time, but to wander around the Serpentine and eat ice cream, and look at the outdoor art exhibition.

"The what?"

"All these artists come out on Sundays and hang their paintings on the park railings. Some of it's terrible – well, most of it really, but there's some good stuff as well. And there are people who do portraits while you wait, or cartoons. That's fun to see."

Mum had to agree that Andie could go, but went through a list of *dos* and *don'ts*, ending with: "*Don't* be back later than six. I mean that, Andie."

"What's with your mum?" Kris asked, as they waited for the bus. "Why's she so strict?"

"Oh, she's just not used to…well, to London. She likes it, but she thinks I'll get lost or kidnapped the second I leave the apartment." Andie felt an uncharacteristic desire to stand up for her mother. "They're a bit disappointed today, Mum and Dad. They went to look at some apartments yesterday, but they turned out to be much too small." And dilapidated, Mum had said, and none too clean, and not in streets she'd want to live in, either. "That's one drawback to staying here in Chelsea Walk," Dad had pointed out. "We're getting used to standards of luxury we'll never afford for ourselves."

"Oh, too bad," Kris sympathized. "I hope you find somewhere fairly close, anyway."

Andie could have told her that there was little chance of that. Real estate agents' details were arriving by mail several times a week, but, as Mum put it, what she could afford she didn't like, and what she liked she couldn't afford. To make it worse, there was an apartment for sale farther along Chelsea Walk, but when Mum had rung to ask the price she had put the phone down again very quickly.

Andie wasn't going to let today be spoiled. She and Kris did some very splashy rowing on the Serpentine, then walked all the way across the park to Speaker's Corner, where, Kris said, anyone could stand up on a box and make a speech. "Only no one's doing it today. Quite often someone's on about the love of God or macrobiotic diets or miners' unions, or whatever they're into. Votes for women, it used to be – did you know a suffragette used to live in your apartment? Even went to prison, Patrick told me. She was Anne

Rutherford's great-aunt or something."

But now here were the paintings, the artists, ranged along the outside of the park fence, so that Bayswater Road had become a linear art gallery. Pictures were hung from the fence or propped against it – landscapes, portraits, fantasy scenes, prints, pastels, oils or delicate watercolors, enamel work, miniatures, models and sculptures, sewn pictures and collages – every kind of artwork Andie could imagine. Most had price labels on them, and were much less expensive than Andie had seen in shops. She looked at the people with interest, because they were artists like her. Some were sitting on the ground, one was even asleep, curled up with her dog on a big cushion, while others tried to chat with passers-by or offered to draw them as caricatures.

Kris had very definite tastes, marching past anything she didn't like, straight to those pictures that caught her eye. The ones she liked best looked Chinese, in bold ink and wash, and somehow gave the effect of sweeping rain.

"If I could paint, that's the sort of thing I'd do," Kris said. "Only there are chimpanzees who can paint better than me. How 'bout you?"

Andie hesitated, then said, "I do paint. Painting's what I do."

Kris looked at her in surprise. "Why didn't you say? I mean, I'm no artist, but I'd like to see your stuff."

"I don't know." Andie wished she'd kept quiet. "I mean – you live with Patrick, a rea— I mean, he's a professional. What I do would seem like fooling around."

"But that's how everyone starts. Trying things. Seeing what works and what doesn't. He does a lot of fooling around himself. You will let me have a look, won't you? Oh, go on! I'd really like to."

"Well, perhaps," Andie said cautiously. Maybe Kris would forget about it, or was only taking a polite interest. But when they got back to Chelsea Walk, and Andie was about to say, "Bye, see you tomorrow," Kris said, "Wait up – what about your paintings? Aren't you going to show me?"

"Well, all right. But only if you don't say anything to Patrick. Promise?"

"Why?"

"I don't like people seeing them. I mean, *you* can – but anyone else, it's kind of too risky. We've got this awful art teacher at school who thinks I'm rubbish, and – if anyone else tells me that, I might start to believe it."

Kris shrugged. "Okay. I promise not to tell you you're rubbish."

"But then," Andie said, newly anxious, "you mustn't say you like them unless you really do!"

"Andie – just get them, will you?"

They went upstairs. Mum was getting tea in the kitchen; Kris chatted with her, in her easy way, while Andie went into the bedroom and took her paintings out of their folder. She hadn't shown these to anyone else: not Prune, not Mum, not Dad. Mum would only say, "Very nice, love," or something as empty as that; Dad might advise her to paint baked-bean cans instead and call it Pop Art.

Andie laid out the paintings on Anne Rutherford's candlewick bedspread, and fetched Kris.

Kris looked at them without speaking, while Andie remembered how critical she'd been of the paintings in the park – giggling, derisive (though not within earshot of the artists), pouring scorn on those she dismissed. I shouldn't have given in, Andie thought. They're mine – private. When someone else looked at them, it was as if the paintings were pinned in the glare of harsh spotlights that showed up all their flaws. She frowned, knowing they weren't good enough. What was it, with her own work? No matter how pleased she was when she'd finished painting, or when she looked at her work last thing at night, it took less than a day to become dull and flat, no better than anyone else could do. Now her moonscapes looked garish and clumsy, the colors too bold, the perspectives all wrong.

"Andie!" Kris finally said, and her voice was full of reproach.

"TARGET MOON" was on the front cover of the *Radio Times*, with a picture of a rocket lifting off. Moon excitement was everywhere; the papers and the TV news were counting down the days to the Apollo 11 launch on Wednesday. The astronauts, Buzz Aldrin, Neil Armstrong and Michael Collins, had to practice being weightless, and moving around in their bulky suits that made them look like space toys. It would take till Sunday for them to reach the moon. How amazing, Andie thought, to be going where no human being had ever been before! Would it change them for ever? How could you fly to the moon, then come back home to ordinary life?

They would collect samples of moon rock and moondust and bring them back to be analyzed. From that, scientists hoped to learn more about how the moon had formed – whether its mountains were really volcanoes, how its craters had been made, whether there was or had ever been water on the moon, and how far it was similar to Earth. The likelihood of the mission succeeding was discussed endlessly. Even if the astronauts landed on the moon, what were the chances of them returning? What if the lunar module simply sank into the moondust and disappeared? Or what if the astronauts *did* come back, but brought deadly bacteria with them?

"Everyone's Gone to the Moon" was being played again and again on the radio. Andie heard the words, over and over in her head, while she worked on her paintings. Although she knew it was silly, she didn't like the thought of *everyone* watching the moon, thinking about it, wondering; it made it less *hers*. The moon would surely prefer to be left alone.

In her pictures, though, she could roam the moon of her imagination.

"Hey," Kris had said, in the bedroom. "You're *good*, Andie! Really good!"

Andie felt herself glowing all over again, remembering. Kris wouldn't say that just to be polite.

Andie was encouraged, and continued painting. Her moonscapes became ever more intricate, their colors more intense. The Earth, reduced to a coin-sized disk in the sky, floated above, casting cool greenish earth-light, reflected from the sun.

Mr. and Mrs. Kapoor invited everyone in the house to a Moon Party on the weekend, which would start late on Sunday night and go on through the early hours of the morning. It seemed likely that TV coverage would continue all night long, so that the moon landing could be shown as it was happening. Andie's head reeled at the idea of TV coming live from the moon – like watching *Dr Who* or *Star Trek*, only this would be real, actually happening, while people all over the world gazed at their television screens.

The semester had finished now at St. Dunstan's, and Sushila was busy helping her mother with fundraising for the charity she worked for. Prune spent her afternoons in the Kapoors' apartment, putting leaflets into envelopes, addressing them and taking bundles to the post office. At least, Andie thought, Prune wasn't likely to get into trouble while she was with sensible Sushila.

Ravi seemed to spend quite a bit of time playing cricket, or practicing with friends, but sometimes Andie saw him in the garden, or coming in through the side gate. Once he was playing chess with Kris under the walnut tree: "But it's so *boring*," Kris said. "He always wins."

While Andie watched, Ravi finished off the game in three decisive moves. "Checkmate *again*!" Kris moaned. "And just when I had something really clever worked out."

Ravi gave one of his shy looks from under his bangs. "But you'd complain if I let you win."

"Well, of course," Kris humphed. "If I win, I want to win properly. Some chance."

Ravi was already putting the chess pieces away in their box. Although Andie had only the most basic idea of chess, she would have liked a turn, if he'd asked; but he only said, "See you later," and went indoors.

"I don't get it," Andie said to Kris. "Sometimes he's friendly, and sometimes he isn't."

Kris smiled. "No, it's not that. He likes to keep his friends in separate compartments. Me for chess, a friend from school for cricket practice, someone else for swimming."

"And, um, me for star-watching, then," Andie confessed. "While you were away, and once before."

Kris didn't seem particularly surprised. "Prowling round the chimneys at night? Moon mania, that's what it is. There's no getting away from it. Even I'm starting to get hooked."

There was more skywatching on Tuesday night. At last, with practice and the help of *The New Astronomer*, Andie was finding more of the skymarks for herself: not just the Big Dipper but the whole of Ursa Major, and Casseiopia, and Lyra and the Summer Triangle. The night sky was changing from a confusing sprinkle of stardust into recognizable constellations and clusters. Soon, though, hazy cloud put an end to gazing, and Ravi unscrewed the telescope from its tripod.

It was Kris's idea that the three of them should go to the Science Museum on Wednesday, to watch the Apollo 11 launch live from America. Ravi must have decided that this was a special enough occasion for him to be with two friends at once, and agreed.

Lots of people had the same idea. Opposite the lift on the first floor, a room was set aside for radio broadcasting, and a demonstration of color television, which Kris and Andie had seen on their first visit. Soon, people who could afford it would have color TV in their own homes, just like going to the movies. But for the moon mission, a much larger screen had been installed, with a direct link to Cape Kennedy. Andie, Kris and Ravi joined the crowd of people – adults and children – who had gathered in the warm, stuffy room, some standing, some sitting on the floor.

The launch tower made Andie think of the Eiffel Tower in Paris. Next to it, tethered and steaming quietly, was the Saturn rocket, elongated and elegant, like something from *Thunderbirds*. The astronauts were already on board, right at the very top, waiting. The television showed them eating their breakfast earlier, steak and eggs and orange juice, looking like people getting ready for an ordinary day at work; then, bulky and padded in their spacesuits, being driven to the launch pad, going up by lift to the command module, and being helped inside.

It would be a while yet. Andie felt too tense to watch any more. What must it be like, belting yourself into the top of a space rocket, knowing that some people estimated their chance of returning as only fifty-fifty? She wandered off with Kris into the adjoining gallery; Ravi wouldn't budge, but stood absorbing every detail.

Excitement mounted as time for the launch drew near, with more and more people packed into the room, those outside getting as close as they could to the doorway. Andie lost Kris altogether in the crush, and could just see Ravi toward the front of the audience. Nothing seemed to be happening, nothing at all, but "Four minutes and counting," said an American voice, unbelievably calm. A countdown began on the screen, stretching out the seconds for longer than felt possible. "Ignition sequence starts – six – five – four – three – two – one – zero –" Andie held her breath and everyone around her seemed to be doing the same; there was the tiniest of pauses before the rocket began to lift. Andie had expected it to soar off at extreme speed, like an exploding firework, and was astonished that it could rise so slowly – more like an elevator going up, she thought, than the great whoosh she'd expected. "All engines running – tower cleared—" and the commentator's voice was drowned by clapping and cheers and exclamations. The rocket was soaring now, with a fiery tail; just a slim, pencil shape.

Everyone's gone to the moon. In their imaginations, anyway. It was hard to think about much else.

Chapter Thirteen

Down to Earth

"Don't go out after supper, girls," Mum said, with her head in the larder. "We need to sit down and talk."

Andie was feeding the cats, Prune helping to put the shopping away. Andie glanced at Prune for a reaction, but got only a shrug in reply. *Sit down and talk?* Last time that happened, it was to tell the girls about the move to Chelsea. Now? Was it about *staying* in London? Had Mum and Dad found their dream apartment or their perfect house? But Mum didn't sound joyful or excited. It was more the tone of voice she'd used after reading Andie's school report – disappointed, resigned.

They had to wait till Dad was home, and they'd eaten cold ham and salad, and canned peaches with cream. Then, when everything was washed up and put away, and the kitchen wiped and scoured to Mum's satisfaction, and coffee made, they all sat around the dining table.

"I'm sorry, girls, but this is going to be a big let-down," Dad began. "Things aren't working out quite as we hoped."

They'd obviously planned this. Dad sounded as if he'd prepared a speech; Mum sat gazing sadly at the tablecloth.

"Your mum and I have been to lots of real estate agents and read all the property pages," Dad went on, "and been to see some apartments, as you know. There's no way round it. We've had to realize that we just can't afford the sort of place we'd like. Either we'd have to settle for some tiny apartment, far too small for the four of us – or live so far out that we may as well stay put, in Slough.

"What?" Prune burst out. "You mean we're just going back home?"

"But what about your job?" Andie asked her father. "That was the whole reason for coming here, wasn't it? You're not going back to your old one?"

"No, no." Dad shook his head. "I'll stay with the new job. *That's* going well, at any rate. I'll just have to commute from Slough every day."

Prune looked disgusted. "But I don't want to go back to boring old Slough! I like it here!"

"I know, love – we all do," said Mum. "But we've got to be practical. We can never afford an apartment like this. We'll just have to enjoy staying here, while it lasts. We've got another two weeks."

"It means there's no need to change schools," Dad added, "and you've both got your friends back at home—"

"I've got friends *here,* now! So's Andie. I want to stay. It's not fair, bringing us here and letting us get used to it, then dragging us back to that dismal dump of a house."

Mum straightened. "Dismal dump? That's our home you're talking about, Prue. Dad and I worked hard to get it. It wasn't easy. We used to *dream* of having a home of our own—"

Prune sighed. "Don't let's start on ancient history!"

"Shut up, Prune!" Andie kicked her under the table; Prune gave a yelp, and glared back. "What's the use of whining?"

Mum sighed. "I did think we could have a sensible *discussion.*"

"What's the point?" snapped Prune. "You've made your minds up, haven't you?"

Dad shook his head. "It's more a question of having our minds made up for us."

So, Andie thought, everything will be back as it was. She'd be back in the navy uniform of Hillsden High, waiting at the bus stop for Barbara each morning. It would be nice to talk and giggle with Barb again, and sit at the back in math where they could pass notes to each other, and take their packed lunches out to the bench by the sports field when it was sunny – but what about Kris and Ravi? They were her new friends. She wanted to see Barbara, but she wanted Ravi and Kris as well, that was the problem.

"You're quiet, Andie," said Dad. "What are you thinking?"

"I – I was thinking about school. I quite liked the idea of going to the same school as Kris."

"But, Andie," Mum said gently. "Mary Burnet is a fee-paying school. We could never afford for you to go there. It would have been St. Dunstan's for you and Prue."

Andie hadn't even thought of that. Everything around her had slumped into dullness – but still, she couldn't see the point of going into a Prune-like sulk. It wasn't Mum and Dad's fault. If they couldn't afford to live in London, they couldn't afford it, and that was that. She glanced around the dining room – at the table that was polished by Maria once a week, at the glass-fronted cabinet full of crystal glasses, at the elegant chairs they were sitting on. We just don't belong in a place like this, she thought. We've only been kidding ourselves, pretending.

"Tell you what," Mum said brightly, "why don't we plan a nice day out for tomorrow? The four of us?"

"Good idea." Dad was trying to sound cheery. "There are lots of tourist things we've not done yet. How about Madame Tussaud's?"

"I don't want a nice day out." Prune sat hunched and defiant. "And I'm definitely not trudging round staring at a lot of stupid waxworks. What's the point?"

Only two days ago, Prune had told Andie that she *wanted* to go to Madame Tussaud's. In this mood, she wasn't likely to be pleased with anything.

"Come on, Prue," Mum tried. "You're not being fair. It's not just a whim, you know, this change of plan –

Dad and I are disappointed too. We really thought we could live in London. But it's just not possible."

"It's not *my* choice, commuting," said Dad. "Setting my alarm for the crack of dawn – waiting for trains – getting home late and tired. But let's be positive. I've still got the job."

"It's not good enough, though," Prune huffed. "It's always money, isn't it? Why's there never enough?"

"Prue! Let's keep a sense of perspective, shall we?" said Dad. "We won't be begging on the streets! We're lucky, when you think about it – *more* than lucky. I'm bringing in a reasonable salary with this new job, your mum's got the skills to find work anywhere, we've got a roof over our heads and a home of our own, and we've got each other. Let's be grateful for all we *have* got, instead of pining for what we can't have."

"Have you finished the lecture?" Prune was getting to her feet. "I'm going to see Sushila."

How was it, Andie wondered, that the moon was a short rocket-hop away, but the move from Slough to

London was too far to be managed? She went down to find Kris, and tell her the news.

"Oh, that's too bad," Kris sympathized. "But surely there's some way round it?"

Andie couldn't think of one. She didn't understand money – how, for people like Patrick and Marilyn and the Kapoors, it didn't seem to be an issue. They just had plenty of it – enough not to be always talking about it, anyway.

"I've never not lived in a city," Kris said. "London or New York. Can't imagine anything else."

Patrick was downstairs in the cellar, working; classical guitar music floated up the steps. I've been living in the same house as an artist, Andie thought, and I've hardly spoken to him. What was he working on? In a brighter mood, she might have asked if they could go down and see – then, maybe, she might mention, or Kris might mention, her own ambitions... "I want to be an artist – I really, really want it, more than anything in the world," she could say, "but my parents don't think I can. What should I do about it?" Whenever she'd imagined this, she'd decided that it could wait till later – till she felt more confident, or had more pictures to show. But now there wouldn't be much later; it was all coming to an end, and soon.

She felt weighed down with gloom. Her dream seemed as unreachable as the most distant stars. In just a few weeks' time, she'd be back in Miss Temple's dreary lessons, in that dull room where even the air seemed gray and tired. Back to the scrubby brushes, the spongy paper and the colors drained of life.

Chapter Fourteen

One Giant Leap

Andie had never stayed up so late – it was past three o'clock in the morning! – and was now watching the TV screen through a haze of tiredness. They were all in the Kapoors' apartment, clustered around the television in chairs and on floor cushions. Everyone was there – Marilyn and Patrick, Kris, all the Millers and all the Kapoors.

The lunar module had landed, and now everyone

was waiting – "the world waits," as the TV commentary kept saying – for the astronauts to emerge, and the first pictures.

"Do you realize," said Mr. Kapoor – he'd asked them to call him Amit, though Andie couldn't quite bring herself to; he was such a quiet, dignified person and seemed to know so much – "that never before have so many people watched the same event at the same time, all around the world?"

"But only those with access to television and electricity," said his wife. "Hundreds of thousands of people haven't got these things, and to those people – if they hear of it at all – this must seem completely irrelevant. But I have to admit, it's very exciting."

"We'll remember this, for the rest of our lives," Dad said solemnly. "It's history in the making."

Ravi, of course, had gone into the shyest of silences, hiding inside himself, the way he did. No one would guess that he had more than a passing interest in what was happening. Why did he have to be so secretive? Andie wondered. But, when she considered it, lots of people had secrets – *she* did. Perhaps everyone needed a secret self, one that was more real and true than the outside everyday self, that other people saw.

"I bet this'll be commonplace by the time you kids are as old as I am," Patrick remarked. "This is the Space Age. There'll be regular sightseeing trips to the moon. Space cruises."

"Holidays on Mars," said Kris. "Vacations on Venus. Count me in!"

"The Russians won't want to be outdone," Dad said. "I bet they'll have men on the moon before long."

"Or women," Sushila added. "One of the first Russian cosmonauts was a woman – Valentina someone."

"Tereshkova," Ravi put in.

"Valentina Tereshkova. That's right."

Kris said, "Who's going to be the first woman on the moon? Why should men have all the fun?"

"I don't agree with all this women's lib stuff," said Mum. "Women wanting to be just the same as the men. Where's it all going to lead?"

Did she *have* to come out with such squirm-making remarks? "Mu-um!" Andie reprimanded, out of the corner of her mouth.

"You'd better not say that too loudly in the upstairs flat," Patrick said, smiling at Mum. "The ghost of Edwina Rutherford might come back to haunt you."

"Edwina Rutherford?"

"Jeremy Rutherford's aunt. It used to be her flat – she left it to him when she died. She was a suffragette – went to prison for it, more than once – very formidable lady, she must have been—"

"Shh! Something's happening –"

Everyone watched the screen, listening, waiting. Andie thought of all the attention focused on these men – Neil Armstrong and Buzz Aldrin, the two who were in the Eagle, and actually on the moon's surface, while Michael Collins stayed in the command module. Poor him! To go all that way, and not make the final descent to the moon! It must be like not being picked for the hockey team, only thousands of times worse. But what if it all went wrong, and he had to return to Earth alone? What if the other two, down on the moon's surface, couldn't take off again, couldn't get back to the command module? What if the first men on the moon were also the first to *die* there? They must be so brave, accepting the huge risks. Like the crew of Apollo 1, who had all died when their rocket exploded on the launch pad...

Snatches of fuzzy conversation could be heard, or sometimes not quite heard, between the module and mission control at Cape Kennedy. Crackly voices – sounding far away, though certainly not a quarter of a million miles away – exchanged remarks and sometimes even jokes. It was Neil Armstrong whose voice had said calmly, "The Eagle has landed," from what was now called Tranquility Base, and who came slowly, blurrily into focus, as *FIRST LIVE PICTURES FROM MOON* came up on the screen. On leaving the capsule, he had lowered a TV camera, which was now – amazingly – sending back images! At first, Andie couldn't tell what she was seeing; it looked like a snowy landscape with some sort of building in the foreground. Then she realized that it was a ladder, and a part of the spidery module, and that the large pale shape moving slowly down was Neil Armstrong himself, stepping carefully just like Dad had done when he wallpapered the lounge. "I'm at the foot of the ladder," he said, speaking to them live from the moon – from the moon itself! "The surface appears to be very, very fine grained as you get close to it – it's almost a powder." He hesitated on the lowest step. "I'm going to step off the ladder." A bigger drop, some fuzzing and blurring, and his voice again: "That's one small step for man, a giant leap for mankind."

Everyone was talking at once. "That's it! Man on the moon!"

"Wow! Unbelievable!"

"They've done it! They're there!"

"The moon's a real *place*! He's standing on it –"

"How must that feel? To stand where no human being has stood before, ever?"

"Amazing! Incredible!"

"*A* man, he must have meant to say," said Sushila. "One small step for *a* man, a giant leap for mankind. Doesn't make sense, otherwise."

They all watched while Neil Armstrong collected samples of moondust and rock. A few minutes later, Buzz Aldrin came carefully down the ladder, guided by Armstrong – bobbing like an inflated toy in the moon's reduced gravity. And now the two were talking to each other: "Isn't that something? Isn't it fine?" It sounded so ordinary; they might have been on the beach at Brighton. Andie had expected them to say something more startling, something wise and wonderful. But what? Perhaps "Wow!" and "Unbelievable!" and "Isn't that something?" were the best that could be done with words, when you saw something utterly astonishing. Perhaps a person standing on the moon wouldn't quite be able to believe what they'd seen and done, till much later. Perhaps not ever.

Neil Armstrong aimed his camera at what he called "the panorama," the view from where he stood – the surface of the moon, pale, flat, pockmarked. But it wasn't Andie's moon. She had the odd feeling that *her* moon was somehow more real. Part of her longed to go back there, by herself.

The two astronauts put up an American flag and posed beside it.

"That doesn't seem right," Sushila said. "It's like they're claiming the moon for America."

"The plaque says *for all mankind*," Kris pointed out.

"I know, so it ought to be an Earth flag. Or no flag at all."

"An Earth flag! Now, that would be something," agreed Sushila's mother. "I can't help thinking that all those billions of dollars this has cost would've been better spent on reducing poverty in Africa and India. It seems dreadful that people starve in Biafra while these colossal sums are spent on landing two men on the moon."

"Shh, shh, here's Richard Nixon."

Now the President of the United States was speaking to the astronauts by telephone from the White House. "This certainly has to be the most historic phone call ever made," he said. "For every American, this has to be the proudest thing of our lives, and for people all over the world." It sounded like he was reading a speech. "Because of what you have done, the heavens have become a part of man's world."

"But they always have been," said Ravi. "People have always looked at the stars, and tried to make sense of them."

He immediately looked embarrassed at having said so much. A few moments later, when his mother went into the kitchen to bring in cakes and sweet pastries and coffee, he followed her out of the room, and didn't come back. Andie guessed that he'd escaped to the attic. She was torn between carrying on watching the television, and following him outside to look at the real moon.

It was Kris who noticed next. "Where's Ravi? I can't believe he's missing this!"

"Gone to bed?" Patrick said, yawning. "It'll be hardly worth it if we stay up much longer."

"If I know Ravi," said Mr. Kapoor, "he'll have gone up to the roof. He's got a telescope now – his uncle gave it to him."

"On the roof?" Mum looked puzzled. "How does he get up to the roof?"

Andie tried not to turn red.

"There's a way out through the attic storeroom. It's quite safe," Mr. Kapoor told her. "You've been up there, I expect, Kris?"

"Sure," Kris answered, then, to Andie, "How about now? I don't think I'm going to bed at all. Coming?"

Andie followed her very quickly, before anyone

could think of a reason why not.

It was already far too light for stargazing. Toward the east, along the river, the sky was pale mauvey-pink, streaked with faint clouds. The low moon was faint, silvery, two-thirds of it in shadow; present even when it appeared to dissolve into daylight. Although it was ridiculous to imagine she'd see the American flag staking its claim across a quarter of a million miles of sky, she felt reassured that the moon looked as pale and untroubled as it always had.

"Did you see them, Rav?" Kris called, as she and Andie emerged onto the walkway.

"Course! I waved at them, and they waved back." But Ravi was removing the telescope from its mount, putting it back in its leather case.

"Hello, day." Kris held out her arms. "It's nice up here, isn't it? I like the feel of the day starting up."

"And not just any day," said Ravi. "It's Monday. Moon-day."

"Happy Moonday! Hey, is this the first real Moonday?

It might look just the same as any other Monday, but it's not."

Kris looked over the parapet. Andie and Ravi looked too, the three of them in a row, gazing down at Chelsea Walk, and beyond it to the Thames. Andie heard the horn of a barge, the cooing of pigeons, traffic on the bridge, and a siren somewhere; she saw the leafy canopy of trees, the grass below; a dog out walking by himself, and strings of lights along the Embankment; she smelled the faintest tang of salt. It all felt fresh and brand new in the cool air of dawn.

She wanted to catch and keep this moment.

But I'll always remember, she thought, even when I'm ancient and a grandmother. The day I stood on the roof with Kris and Ravi, and watched London wake up, and there were men on the moon.

CHAPTER FIFTEEN

The Slough of Despond

"MAN ON THE MOON" dominated the news. Andie saw the same photographs again and again: the boot-print, heavily shadowed; the Earth from the moon; the two astronauts by the American flag; and Neil Armstrong reflected in Buzz Aldrin's helmet visor. The lunar module had successfully taken off from the surface and – amazingly – docked with the command module exactly as planned, and the first men on the moon were on their way back to Earth.

Andie went back to her own imagined landscapes, where the moon was silent and alone, not the focus of the world's obsessive gaze. She painted the Sea of Tranquility empty once more, with a blur of footmarks, and the prints left by the spidery lunar module; beyond, the powdery surface was unmarked by humans.

On Tuesday she went with Kris to the King's Road, to deliver a batch of Marilyn's jewelry to East of the Sun, West of the Moon. She hoped Zak wouldn't be there – hadn't he said he was only helping out a friend? But he was outside, hanging T-shirts on a rail. He said, "Hi, you guys," mainly to Kris, then looked at Andie as if he recognized her from the shoplifting incident. All her family members, wherever they went, seemed to devote themselves to creating maximum embarrassment for her, Andie thought.

Kris handed over the box of jewelry to the sharp-faced blonde woman and spent a few minutes discussing which of Marilyn's pieces were selling best. As they left the arcade, Zak, who was now at the register, said to Andie, "Tell Prue I got her message, would you? Tomorrow's cool. Quarter to nine, tell her."

"What's that about?" Kris asked, out on the sidewalk.

"No idea." Andie was baffled. "We went in there last week, and Prune, um, talked to Zak. I don't know what else."

"What, is she going out with him or something? That's neat."

Andie thought this most unlikely, but was reluctant to explain why. She'd cross-examine Prune about it later.

Much of the world might have been gazing at the moon, but the King's Road was still the center of its own universe: self-absorbed, inhabited by beautiful people with swishy hair and arty clothes. Where did they come from? Andie wondered. Where did they go to? Had they been bred specially from shop mannequins, or designed by the editors of *Honey*? Somehow, in the King's Road, even the plainest people, simply by being there, managed to make themselves look like the last word in cool.

Walking its length in Kris's company was at least less exhausting than with Prune, who wanted to dive into every shop and exclaim over every window display. Kris, though younger, had an air of having seen it all before, of being used to nothing else. It was Andie who wanted to stop and gaze, and who thought she glimpsed George Harrison in a passing taxi.

"It was *him*! I'm certain!"

"It wasn't!"

"It was!"

With a twinge of regret, Andie knew that she'd miss this. Slough High Street couldn't possibly match this daily parade of hipness and gorgeousness.

They were approaching the Town Hall. Standing squarely over the passers-by, the building made Andie think of a portly great-uncle with twirling mustaches, who had wandered by mistake into a disco. With its grand steps, pillared entrance and gilded clock, it looked surprised to find itself at the heart of fashion-conscious Chelsea. The gallery next door had a noticeboard outside: FASHIONS FOR THE SPACE AGE. EXHIBITION INSIDE.

"Hey, see this?" she called to Kris, who was about to walk on past.

They stopped to read. The poster gave details of a summer vacation competition, open to anyone under eighteen; entries were being displayed from now until the end of July.

"Shall we?"

"Sure, why not?"

They went inside. The gallery consisted of several rooms, one of which, light and airy, displayed the competition entries. Pictures and paintings were mounted on the walls, and on screens reaching across the middle. The work was of varying skill – some could easily have come from fashion magazines;

some were clumsily drawn in colored pencil or pastel. The concept of "The Space Age" had been given wide interpretation, from spacesuits like the ones the Apollo astronauts wore, to designs inspired by Mary Quant or Biba.

"Looks like fun," Kris was saying. "You ought to have a go at this, Andie – it's not too late, is it? Why not?"

Andie stopped dead, staring. There, on a screen in front of her, were three of her own fashion drawings – mounted on card, neatly labelled, each one signed in a flourishing hand by *Prue Miller.*

"They're cool," said Kris. "See, you could do as well as that – Hey, *Prue Miller*! Is that your Prune? I didn't know she was into drawing, as well?"

"She isn't." Andie's voice came out strangled.

Kris raised her eybrows. "They look pretty good to me."

"But they're *mine*! The ideas are hers, the clothes. *I* drew them – to cheer her up – but she never told me – the lying cow!"

Kris seemed to find this amusing. "Well, I guess you'll be letting her know what you think about that."

"You can say that again!"

"Do you think you could have your argument out on the street?" A woman's face appeared around one end of the screen, and a curly-haired toddler ducked underneath to peer at the girls, round-eyed. "Some of us are trying to enjoy the exhibition."

"Sorry." Andie hadn't realized there was someone else in the room. "But how *could* she?" she hissed at Kris. "Put *her* signature on *my* drawings! It's fraud, that's what it is!"

She stared at the drawings in indecision, half inclined to rip them off the display board. But part of her was *proud* to have work on show in an exhibition in the King's Road, even if it was just a larky summer vacation thing. The cheek of Prune, though!

"It'd be worse," Kris pointed out, "if she'd taken your paintings. Your moon pictures. I mean, these are good, but they're not really *you*, like the others are."

Andie wouldn't be pacified. It was still outrageous. It was practically *theft*.

"May as well take a look at the rest, now we're here," said Kris.

The drawings and paintings passed before Andie's eyes in a blur of color and line. She was impatient to get home, and let out the pressure that was building up inside her till she felt jet-propelled with anger and indignation.

"Prune? Prune, you in?" she shouted, letting herself into the apartment.

No answer. Typical of Prune not to be around when she was wanted. Now what?

Andie ran downstairs and out to the garden, looking for Kris. And there Prune was – on the swing, swaying gently back and forth.

"Prune? What are you doing?" Andie yelled.

Prune looked up vaguely. "Waiting for Sushila."

"Oh. And then what are you doing? Going to look at

the exhibition next to the Town Hall, by any chance?"

"I don't know what you're talking about," said Prune, but the pinking of her cheeks gave her away.

"Yes, you do. Three drawings signed by *Prue Miller.* Three of *my* drawings. Signed themselves, did they? Entered themselves for the competition?"

"Oh," said Prune. "Those."

"Yes, *those.* How could you do it, Prune? How could you be so sneaky? Why didn't you *ask*?"

"They were my ideas." Prune looked at her defiantly. "You wouldn't have done it otherwise. You only did the drawing."

"*Only!* What do you mean, *only*?"

"Oh, don't be so mean, Andie! You know how much I want to work in fashion. If I win that competition—"

"If *you* win it!" Andie humphed. "Some chance! Did you look at the other entries? There are loads better than yours – I mean *mine.* How could you be so sneaky, entering my drawings with your name on them!

You didn't even ask – didn't think that we could *both* have entered – didn't say a word!" She paused for breath, and relaunched. "That's just typical of you! Whatever you want, you think you can help yourself – like that bangle, and the Biba dress—"

"Stop it, Andie!" Prune stood up, red-faced. "Don't keep going on at me! It was just a mistake, you know, in the shop, and—"

"Huh! And I suppose *this* was a mistake! Signing my pictures, and taking them to the exhibition? Don't make me laugh—"

"What on earth's going on?"

The big male voice shocked them both into silence. It was Patrick, standing at the top of the basement steps.

"I said what's going on? It sounds like a wild-cat-fight's broken out. Can't you go upstairs and have your squabble?"

He was talking in his usual mild way, but there was a sternness behind it that made Andie feel intimidated.

"Oh – nothing," she faltered.

"Didn't sound like nothing. What's all this about someone signing someone else's pictures?"

Kris had come up the steps behind him. Everyone was looking at everyone else; no one was talking.

"It's – a bit complicated." Andie was first to break the silence.

"Well, cool it, will you? You're like a pair of parrots, screeching away. It's too warm inside to have the doors closed, and believe it or not, I'm trying to *work.*" He turned, bumped into Kris, and went back down the steps.

"Sorry!" Andie called after him.

Kris made a rueful face, and followed. Prune and Andie, very aloof with each other, went up to the apartment.

As if Prune hadn't done enough already! Andie grumped to herself. Now Patrick, who she wanted so hard to impress, thought she was a squawking parrot, a raucous nuisance.

Eventually, Prune made the first move, coming into the bedroom, where Andie sat icily by the window with her sketchbook. "Listen, And. Why don't we go there, to the gallery? Then you can cross out my name and put yours, and we can ask for the entry form back and put your name on that as well."

"You go," Andie mumbled. "I can't be bothered."

Still, it was the nearest thing to *sorry* she was likely to get from Prune. And only now did she remember the message she was supposed to pass on. "I saw Zak this morning. He said fine for tomorrow, quarter to nine. What's that about? Is it a date, or what?"

"A date? No!" Prune laughed, then gave her a furtive look. "I've got a job there. I'm going to help out two days a week, Thursdays and Saturdays. Or at least I *was* – I said I'd do it for the whole summer vacation, only now how can I, when we're going back home a week from Friday?"

"Didn't you think of that?"

"Course I did, Miss Smartypants, only I thought

something would turn up. And it doesn't look like it will. We're heading back to the Slough of Despond."

Andie looked at her. "How did it happen, then, getting the job? I mean, last time we were in there, you—"

"I know," Prune said defensively. "Tried to shoplift. You're going to say I'm the last person they'd want working there. But I liked Zak – he was funny and nice, and he didn't turn me in to Alicia – that's the manager, the woman we saw – when he easily could have. So I went back to say thank you, and – and that it *wasn't* a mistake, but I wouldn't do it again. And then he asked if I'd like to help out. I've got a job, Andie! A job in the King's Road! It's a start, isn't it?"

"I wouldn't get too excited. You'll be there three days before we go home."

Later, while Andie was washing up the cat dishes and Mum and Dad were watching *Man Alive* on TV, Kris came up.

"Will you do me a favor? No, what I mean is,

will you do yourself a favor?"

"Sure," Andie said, surprised. "What?"

"Come down and show Patrick your paintings. Your moon paintings."

Andie was suspicious. "Why?"

"Well –" Kris was unwisely trying to cuddle Rumpelteazer, who yowled, and stalked away in indignation – "I told him why you argued with Prune. And I told him about your paintings and how good they are. And he said he'd like to see them."

Andie shook her head. "No! He'll think they're rubbish."

"Up to you." Kris threw both hands up. "Have it your way. Don't bother talking to Patrick, who's – well, I'm not saying he's a genius, but he's *good,* and he makes a living from it, and he teaches students and he knows when someone's got it and when they haven't, but never mind what he thinks. Go back to your dreary old art teacher, and let her tell you whether you can paint or not. Is that what you want?

“No –”

“Right. So let’s go.”

Chapter Sixteen

Splashdown

Andie wished she had something better than a cardboard folder held together with string, something more likely to impress Patrick – but she needn't have worried. By the time she and Kris got down to the cellar, he was nowhere to be seen.

"Oh, sorry!" Marilyn said, when they trooped back up to the kitchen, where she was slicing a pineapple. "Doug turned up unexpectedly, and they've gone to the Pheasantry to meet this record producer. Doug's his agent," she explained to Andie. "And it looks like a big contract might come out of this, so they've got a lot to talk about – I shouldn't think he'll be back till late. Oh, and you wanted to show him your pictures – what a shame!"

She sounded, Andie thought, like a kindly teacher encouraging an infant. But she didn't say that *she* wanted to see the paintings. Andie tucked the folder more firmly under her arm, wanting to hide it from view.

"Doesn't matter," she said, half-heartedly. She'd take it back upstairs where it belonged, hidden behind the armoire.

"No, leave it." Kris pried the folder from Andie's grip. "He can look tomorrow."

While Andie fretted and fidgeted about not having her paintings in their usual hiding place, Prune erupted into the apartment with good news.

"I can stay at Sushila's! Stay here for a whole two weeks. I needn't go back home with you!"

"What's this about?" Dad was reading the newspaper, Mum ironing one of his striped shirts.

Prune babbled it out. She was going to carry on helping Mrs. Kapoor with her charity fundraising – there was a special day of speeches and talks coming up at the Town Hall in the middle of August, and Sushila was doing part of the organizing, and Prune would help, too – and she had her part-time job at East of the Sun, West of the Moon, so she'd be earning her own money, and Mr. and Mrs. Kapoor said she was welcome to stay with them, and it would be great, and Mum and Dad couldn't possibly object, could they? Not when she'd be doing something so *useful.*

"Well, I don't know." Mum was wearing her cautious expression. "I'd need to talk to the Kapoors myself. Are you sure that's what they said? And the middle of August? That's when your exam results come out. It'll be time to make decisions about your future. You'll need to be enrolled somewhere – we've put it off too long already."

"That's all right – I'll be home by then. And I've more or less decided to stay on at school, if my grades are good enough. Go on, Mum! Dad! Say yes – I want to, *so much* –"

"Well, I can't see why not, as long as—" Dad began.

"What's this about a part-time job?" Mum interrupted.

Just turned midnight, and Andie was wide awake.

A week from now would be their last night at Number Six, Chelsea Walk. No more Kris. No more Ravi. No more King's Road. No more London on their doorstep, with all its excitement.

No more skywatching. Well, she could still *watch* the sky, of course; she could stand out in the back garden and look at the stars, but it wouldn't be the same without Ravi and his telescope and his knowledge.

Nor would it be the same as being up high in the London rooftops, picking out landmarks.

What was she doing, lying in bed now, wasting precious time? She hadn't heard Ravi go up – no telltale creaking above her head – but he might be there, all the same.

She put on sandals and a sweater, and crept out of the apartment and up the attic stairs, tuning her ears to the silence. It was funny how silences could vary. There was the almost tingling silence when you knew something would happen, someone was there – like that first time. And then the really silent silence that meant only emptiness. The whole house was sleeping, and Andie knew, before tiptoeing past the maids' rooms and through the storeroom to the low door that led out, that Ravi wasn't there. The door was locked.

Well, he didn't come up here every night – she knew that. But all the same she felt hollow with disappointment. She went back down, and got into bed, and lay there hot and resentful as she listened to

Prune's steady breathing. Everything was working out for Prune, wasn't it? Mum and Dad had agreed that she could stay on with Sushila, and even seemed pleased at her initiative in getting the shop job. So Prune had got what she wanted, and it didn't seem at all fair, to Andie.

She thought of her worn folder, down in Patrick's apartment, and felt uneasy, wishing she hadn't left it there. First thing tomorrow, she'd go down and fetch it back.

The basement doors were open. Andie went down, hearing a voice inside; but it was Marilyn, talking on the phone at her bench. There was no sign of Kris, nor of Patrick, and Andie remembered now that Kris was spending the day at a drama workshop.

"Hang on a minute." Marilyn lowered the receiver. "Have you come for your folder, Andie? It's over there." She smiled and nodded, and went back to her conversation.

The folder was lying on a drafting table on Patrick's side of the room. Andie grabbed it, and clutched it to her chest. Was that all, then? Had Patrick even bothered to look? Perhaps he had, and thought her work was awful – too childish to waste his time on.

Out in the garden, she flipped it open and had a quick look inside, thinking he might have left a note, even just a *Not bad* or a *Thank you*.

Nothing. He must think it was so awful that he couldn't think of anything to say.

SPLASHDOWN DAY FOR APOLLO MOON MEN was all over today's paper; but even this excitement couldn't brighten Andie's spirits. She didn't want to look at her paintings, let alone do any more. She wandered aimlessly along the Embankment, then returned to flick aimlessly through the pages of a book. In such a slump as this, nothing seemed worth doing; with no way to cast it off, she may as well let herself wallow. There was no one around to notice, with Mum and Dad and now Prune all out at work for the day. Mungojerrie seemed delighted that she was so miserable, and lay alongside her, warm and purry. "Typical!" she told him. "You've decided you actually *like* me now, I suppose? Now that I'm nearly going home?" The Slough of Despond awaited, and maybe it was the best place for her.

Time dragged by. It was a still afternoon, the sun shining hotly through the bedroom window; it would be cooler in the garden, but Andie couldn't summon the will to move. She was annoyed with herself, but unable to do anything about it. How stupid to be wasting what little was left of her time in London!

She didn't even stir from the bed when at last a key turned in the lock of the front door.

"Come on down, And!" Prune burst into the bedroom, looking in the best of moods. One day at East of the Sun, West of the Moon, and already she looked a little less dolly-bird and a bit more Zak-like, in jeans and a patchwork vest, with a small bell on a chain around her neck.

"What's happened to you?" Andie mustered enough interest to prop herself on one elbow.

"Nothing – only everyone's down in the garden, and Patrick's opening champagne. He's got something to celebrate, he says – it's like another party!"

"Mum won't let me drink champagne," Andie grumphed, and almost added that she wasn't coming down, and had never felt less partyish, but curiosity got the better of her. She could always come back up.

Chapter Seventeen

Sparkles

Outside, everyone was sitting on deckchairs or on the grass, while Ravi had the swing. A folding table held bottles of champagne, soda, and wide glasses; Patrick was pouring, and Kris handing around the drinks.

"Well, who knows?" Patrick was saying. "You can never tell, with these rock groups – they come and go. But this bunch have really got something, in my opinion."

Mum turned around and smiled. "Oh, you're here, love. That's good."

Kris handed a glass of soda to Andie. Dad was there as well, tie loosened, suit jacket slung over the back of a deckchair. Music floated up from the basement – something electronic and spacey that sent tingles down the back of Andie's neck.

"What's going on?" she asked Kris.

"It's fantastic! Patrick's got a contract to do album covers for Legend – you know? – to give them a special look that everyone'll recognize. It's big money – the record company's really investing in them –"

"– yes, there's a feature on them in the *New Musical Express* – they're playing at the Isle of Wight next month – that's right, the rock festival – then touring the States –" Patrick was telling everyone.

"Is this them?" Andie asked Kris, meaning the music.

"Yes, aren't they fab? We'll go inside in a minute, and I'll show you the artwork. You'll love it."

In all the excitement, Kris seemed to have forgotten

entirely about showing Andie's paintings to Patrick. Andie nursed a small ache of resentment that promised to swell into a rage of self-pity as soon as she was alone.

Now everyone had a glass, and Marilyn called out, "Here's to Patrick – and Legend!"

"To Patrick!"

"I'm so proud of you, darling –"

"Congratulations – well done!"

Andie took a gulp of soda, too much at once – the fizz erupted sneezily in her nose, and she doubled over, spluttering. Mum looked at her in dismay, and reached across to take the glass.

Only now, for the first time, did Patrick look at her. "Here she is! When she's quite finished choking – give her back that fizz, Maureen – we're all going to raise our glasses again, to this young lady here."

Andie recovered enough to look around the group for a young lady she couldn't have noticed, then realized with a jolt that he meant *her*.

"Andie." Patrick raised his glass to her. "You've certainly got a future as an artist, if you choose to take it. To Andie Miller, everyone – a name you're likely to hear more of –"

Kris was grinning widely. "Told you!"

"Oh! You really think so, do you?" Dad said to Patrick, looking bemused. "I always thought she was quite good – but what do I know? Art, these days – but she's never without her sketchbook and her paints –"

"She's always wanted to be an artist," Mum said doubtfully, "ever since she was little –"

"Well," said Patrick, "she *is* an artist."

Now all the faces were turned Andie's way, and it was like blinking in the beam of a spotlight.

"Are you sure?" Her voice came out as a squawk.

"Sure? I've got final-year students with less talent."

"That's very kind of you, Patrick." Mum was prim and pink, though there was no mistaking her look of pride.

"No, he's not being *kind*," Marilyn told her. "He's

never kind. You should ask some of his students, the ones who crawl away in tears and shred up their work into microscopic bits. He never praises anyone's work unless he really means it."

Andie was giddy with bewilderment "I'd love to be an art student. More than anything in the world."

"No reason why you shouldn't," Patrick said.

Andie shot a defiant look at Mum, who registered it, and explained to Patrick, "We've always encouraged her to think of it as a hobby, haven't we, Dennis? But, well –"

"There's obviously money to be made – prospects – if you know your way around," Dad said. "It doesn't have to be starving in a garret."

"There's plenty of us who have done a stint of *that*, before making much progress," said Patrick. "I'm not saying it's easy – but if you've got talent, and determination – and it seems to me that Andie's got plenty of both – then good luck to you."

Now *everyone* wanted to see Andie's pictures. She

had to bring them down, and suffer the embarrassment of having them looked at and exclaimed over: "That's fantastic, Andie!"..."What an imagination – I feel like I'm actually on the moon –"..."Well! We've always known she *liked* painting, and her teacher says she's got talent..."..."Talent! I should say so!" So many compliments! She thought her head would burst.

Needing to recover, she went inside with Kris to look at Patrick's artwork for the album covers.

Kris opened a portfolio – larger and smarter, as well as much fuller, than Andie's, but she didn't mind that now.

First, there was just the word *LEGEND*, in letters that twined through and around each other like sinuous plants.

"That's going to be their logo – it means like a trademark," Kris explained. "It'll be on the record labels, and on all their posters. They haven't decided which colors yet. And here are the sketches, and this is what they're most likely using for the first album."

Andie looked. It was a fantastical landscape – the sort of thing she might try to paint herself. Picturesque, but also faintly sinister, with towering cliffs and the black clefts of chasms, and precipitous paths, and dark forests. She imagined herself walking into it, and wondered who she might meet.

"It's kind of fairy-tale," she said at last. "Only a *serious* fairy-tale."

"What's to say," said Kris, "that fairy-tales can't be serious? Some of them are *very* serious."

Chapter Eighteen

We Are Stardust

On Wednesday, the Millers' last night at Chelsea Walk, Mum finally plucked up courage to invite everyone in. She had finished her agency work on Friday, and spent all day Monday cleaning the apartment. Tuesday was for shopping – Andie helped – and Wednesday for packing and cooking. They prepared sausages on sticks and quiche. They made egg salad and filled vol-au-vents with mushroom and ham; Mum made her specialty, lemon meringue pie.

Being so busy – even if she thought Mum was going to far more trouble than was necessary – stopped Andie from feeling too sad. All the same, several times she found herself thinking, *This is the last time. Tonight will be the last time I sleep here. The last time I live in the same house as a real artist, and Ravi and Kris. The last time I swing from the walnut tree.*

"Do you think there's enough?" When everything was ready, Mum stood back and surveyed the dining table.

"Mum! If fifteen extra people turned up, we'd *still* have enough."

Mum laughed. "It's fun, though, isn't it? I know I get myself too wound up, but I *like* this. We ought to do it more often, have people round. People at home, I mean. They've been so friendly, haven't they, Patrick and Marilyn and the Kapoors? I hope you're not too disappointed, Andie, this not working out."

Sometimes Andie felt that Mum was too busy

fussing to take proper notice of her; but now Mum had stopped folding napkins, and was looking at her very seriously.

"Well, a bit," Andie said. "But there are nice things about going back home. There's Barbara, and not having to share with Prune. Even not having to change schools."

"I know. I like it here, but I'm looking forward to being back in our own home. But it hasn't been a wasted summer for you here, has it? Making friends with Kris and Ravi, and Patrick thinking so highly of you. He obviously knows what he's talking about. The thing is, me and Dad don't know anything about painting and art. It's another world, to us. But we shouldn't stand in your way, if that's where you want to go. We were talking about it last night. We're very proud of you."

She gave Andie a hug. Automatically, Andie wiggled away; she managed a gruff, "Thanks, Mum. That's great."

Had Mum really said that? What was going on – everyone saying such nice things? Andie thought of Patrick's words as fantastic shiny presents which she could keep unwrapping over and over again.

Wasted summer? How could it have been? Not only had an artist – a real artist – admired her work, but these few weeks had shown her the moon and the stars, the immensity and the mystery. The wonder. And she would always have that, whenever she looked up at the sky on a clear night.

It wasn't as if she was losing her new friends, either. "Slough isn't a million miles away," Ravi had said. "You can come up on the train, can't you? We'll go to the Science Museum again, and the Planetarium, and Madame Tussaud's, and the Geological Museum, and the Zoo."

"Come on a Saturday, and we'll all go see a film," added Kris.

And Prune would be here for another two weeks.

Now that they were going to be separated, Andie felt – rather to her own surprise – that she would actually *miss* Prune.

"Prune? If you want to do any more fashion designs, I don't mind drawing them for you," she offered. "As long as – you know."

"Thanks," said Prune, "but I'm going to be a bit busy for now, with my job and everything. Still, that's nice of you." After a moment, she added: "Do you think you could stop calling me Prune now? You know I don't like it."

This seemed fair enough; Andie agreed. "It'll be hard. But I'll try."

Ravi had spent the last two weeks making a cassette tape of all the songs he could find that were about space or the moon, and it was playing now: "Bad Moon Rising," "Space Oddity," "In the Year 2525." As usual, the grown-ups ate and drank and chatted, but there was only one thing Andie really wanted to do.

As soon as it was dark enough, Ravi fetched his telescope, and he, Kris and Andie went up to the roof. *One last time,* went through Andie's head like a refrain, as they climbed the narrow stairs and went through the storeroom and out.

There it was, the moon. Alone again. Pale, almost transparent, above the glow of London. But of course it wasn't really transparent. It was a place.

"It's still hard to believe, isn't it?"

They were taking turns with the telescope.

"From now on," said Andie, "it'll be Dad's binoculars in the back garden. But at least I've got my skymarks."

"Your dad's binoculars are probably as powerful as Galileo's telescope," said Ravi. "And with that he saw the moons of Jupiter."

"What would he have thought of people flying to the moon?" Kris wondered.

"What would my great-grandmother have thought?" said Ravi. "When she came from India, Queen Victoria was still alive and there were horse-drawn carriages in the streets. But that's like a split second ago, when you think of stars shining at us from hundreds of thousands of light years away."

"It makes us seem so tiny and unimportant," said Andie. "Like specks of dust."

"We *are* specks of dust," Ravi told her. "That's what we're made of. Stardust."

"Oh! You mean, like in the 'Woodstock' song?" Kris started to sing it, in a warbling voice.

"That's right! We've got to be made of the same stuff as stars – whatever it was that exploded when the universe began. Because what else *is* there for us to be made of?"

"But – all of this?" Andie stretched out her hands – to the street below, the traffic, the Albert Bridge, to the rest of London on the other side of the river.

"Everything. Everything there is. The same beginning," said Ravi. Then he clapped his hands over his ears and turned on Kris, who was making a contorted face as she strained for the highest notes. "Is someone strangling a hyena? You're making my brain hurt!"

"See, Andie?" Kris broke off singing. "You don't have to want to be a star, with your painting. You *are* one, already. We all are."

Andie had been about to say, "It's impossible! Everything made of stars?"

But *lots* of things seemed impossible, and not all of them were. Humans had been to the moon, and left footprints, and come back again. There were two people alive who had stood on another world.

If that was possible, who could say what wasn't?

Author's Note

No astronaut has set foot on the moon since 1972, though early this year a Chinese mission landed a spacecraft on the far side: another first. Back in 1969, it was confidently expected that the first exciting steps on the moon would lead to great advances in space travel for humans – but, so far, no habitable base has been set up on the lunar surface. I like to think, though, that during my lifetime we'll see the first woman on the moon. Who will she be, and where will she come from? She may be a child now, growing up with no idea that she'll make history.

The Apollo missions produced, almost by accident, a beautiful photograph that's come to symbolize how precious and fragile our planet is. It's the photograph called Earthrise, which you can easily find online and in many books, taken by astronaut Bill Anders on

Christmas Eve 1968 while orbiting the moon. There's our planet seen as never before, a small blue traveler in the vast silence of space. In the fifty years since Neil Armstrong set foot on the moon, we've done serious damage to that vital atmosphere on which all life depends, through pollution and deforestation and by simply failing to realize the dangers of interfering with ecosystems. All this damage has been done in a frighteningly short time, and we know now that we can't go on ignoring it.

In those years, too, there's been increasing evidence for the likelihood of life elsewhere in the universe. But I hope we won't send humans to live on other planets until we've learned to respect and care for our own.

Meanwhile, I hope you'll enjoy visiting 1969 and the heady excitement of those first footsteps on a place beyond Earth.

Linda Newbery

February 2019

About the Author

Linda has written many books for children, teenagers and adults. She won the Costa Children's Book Prize for *Set in Stone*, and has twice been shortlisted for the Carnegie Medal. With Yvonne Coppard she has written *Writing Children's Fiction: a Writers' and Artists' Companion*, and she runs a review blog, *Writers Review*, with Adèle Geras and Celia Rees, and help from many of their writer friends (including Ann Turnbull).

Linda lives in a small village in Oxfordshire and loves yoga, wildlife, photography, gardening and reading.

See more at *www.lindanewbery.co.uk*

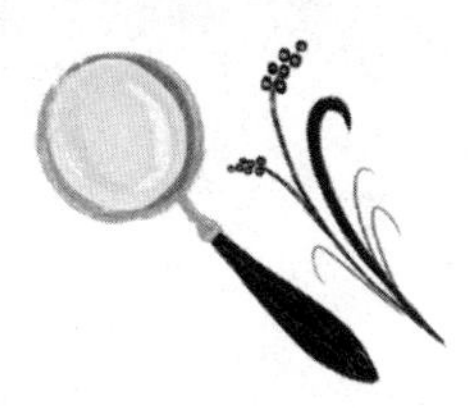

USBORNE QUICKLINKS

For links to websites where you can find out more about Apollo 11's mission to the moon, and fashion and music in 1960s London, go to the Usborne Quicklinks website at www.usborne.com/quicklinks and type in the title of this book.

At Usborne Quicklinks you can:

- Follow highlights of Apollo 11's trip to the moon and see Neil Armstrong's "giant leap"
- Look at Bill Anders's "Earthrise" photograph
- Find out how to spot the Big Dipper, or the Plough, in the night sky
- See mini dresses by Mary Quant and other fashion designers

Please follow the internet safety guidelines at the Usborne Quicklinks website. Children should be supervised online.